GOLD BY GEMINI

A JOAN KAHN BOOK

GOLD  BY GEMINI

By Jonathan Gash

HARPER & ROW, PUBLISHERS

NEW YORK, HAGERSTOWN
SAN FRANCISCO
LONDON

Mystery
Gas

This work was first published in England under the title *Gold from Gemini.*

FIRST U.S. EDITION

Designer: Sidney Feinberg

Library of Congress Cataloging in Publication Data

Gash, Jonathan.
  Gold by Gemini.
  "A Joan Kahn book."
  I. Title.
PZ4.G2468G0   1979   (PR6057.A728)   823'.9'14
ISBN 0-06-011463-0   78-20205

79 80 81 82 83 84 10 9 8 7 6 5 4 3 2 1

Note: The opinion of History is that the Romans did not garrison the Isle of Man, and certainly major finds have not been made. Current belief is that Suetonius did not occupy the island, but instead stormed Anglesey.

The author chooses not to trust History on this point, believing like Lovejoy that faith is sometimes preferable to evidence.

1

Antiques is a lovely but murderous game.

Some bits of this story you won't like. I'm telling you now just in case, but that's the way it is in the world of antiques. It's crammed with love, fear, greed, death, hate and ecstasy. I should know—I'm an antique dealer. And don't chuck this book away in disgust just because I've owned up and told you the truth.

I'm the only person in it you can trust.

*

I was with Brenda on her sofa.

For nearly a month I'd been scouring the surrounding villages without even a sniff of an antique except for a ninth-rate copy of a Norwich School painting, and a Bingham—imagine a blue glaze on the daftest exotic porcelain dreamed up in a nightmare—and I'd had to sweat blood for those. Both were left for collecting later. Both were still unpaid for.

The knack is to look fresh and casual when the woman (ten to one it's a woman) opens the door. I've only one suit I try to jazz up with a splash of red, a plastic flower. Then I knock and give them my patter smiling like an ape.

On the day this story begins I had staggered my way from knocker to knocker, sofa to sofa, my bladder awash with coffee, my mouth sore from snogging, my pockets crammed with phone numbers and dates, but life undeniably grim. Antiques seemed to have vanished from the earth. And they are everything. Everything.

Women and antiques are very similar—they come either in epidemics or not at all. Where all this starts I was in the middle of an epidemic of women, and an antiques drought. The situation was really serious.

When you think of it, making love is rather like picking blackberries from a dense and tangly hedge. You need both hands and a lot of skill to do it properly and get away unscathed, yet your mind can be miles away. As long as you're up to the job in hand, as it were, you need not really concentrate very much. And none of this how-about-her-tenderest-emotions jazz. All the blackberry knows is it's being picked. If it's being picked properly, that is. Preferably by me. And as for me, well, I can only think yippee.

This particular blackberry's name was Brenda, a real goer. Her husband was out—wonderful what a taste of treachery does for the appetite. And it was beautiful, heavenly, ecstasy.

It was even better than that, because from where we were, er, positioned, I had a perfect close-up view of the antique painting on her wall.

I could hardly keep my eyes off it.

*

We were downstairs in her living room. Only lovers get the bedroom, and only idiots go up there unless there's a good reason, such as a granny nodding off in the kitchen or a baby somewhere which mustn't be disturbed. Wandering antique dealers like me get gratification at ground level as a reminder that the affair is temporary. That doesn't mean temporary's bad or even brief. It can be marvellous, like on Brenda's sofa.

But this picture.

If the picture hadn't been clearly visible from her front door I would already have been halfway up the next street. I was just beginning to fear I was losing my touch when she'd hauled me in and started ravishing. She shyly drew the curtains, really quaint.

A glimpse set my heart pounding (I mean the picture, folks, the picture). It seemed really genuine late Carolean. A dark, splendid canvas. Original, too, but somehow.... A smiling woman was presenting a little boy to his father in "cavalier" dress while adoring yokels grovelled in the background. The painting's composition was right. The dresses were accurate. Most dealers would have leapt at it. Not me.

"Oh, God," Brenda moaned, eyes closed and brow damp.

It was a superb forgery. Quality. The canvas I knew would be authentic, not just modern and aged by alternately oven-heating and fan-drying. (A penniless young Austrian painter perfected this particular method when forging pathetically bad copies of Old Masters. Name: Adolf Hitler. He eventually packed it in and turned to other interests.) I guessed the stretcher would be seventeenth century, though naturally pinched. After all, you don't spoil the ship for a ha'porth of tar. Brenda lurched and shuddered. Puzzled, I loved on.

It was in our climax that it hit me, maybe from the exploding colors in my mind. The lady's dress had a graceful crenulated peplum of citrus *yellow,* a clear yet quite witty giveaway. Yellows have been in since Roman days, but citrus yellow's essentially a modern color. I'm quite fond of yellows. While Brenda and I geared down to that quiescent afterglow in which the woman murmurs and the man dreams, I couldn't help wondering what genius had executed a brilliant forgery and then betrayed his work with such knowing elegance. Talent like that doesn't get a whole color wrong. So it was wit, but expensive wit. He could have bought a new yacht with the proceeds. Honesty can be very inconvenient. Still, I liked him, whoever he was. Certainly I couldn't have done a better forgery. I know because I've tried.

She made us coffee afterward, working steadily toward getting my name the way they do. She laughed at Lovejoy (not the first) but you can't forget Lovejoy Antiques, Inc., can you? It sounds huge and expensive American. It's actually only me and three sets of different phoney visiting cards saying that I'm from Christie's, Sotheby's and the National Gallery. People will believe anything. Never mind what the man said. You *can* fool all of the people all of the time. It's practically my job.

3

"You have good taste," I told her.

"Really?" She blossomed. "I got the curtains from—"

"In antiques," I said firmly, refusing to be sidetracked. "That lovely picture, for instance." Casually I crossed to see it. I'd earned the right.

"Are you married, Lovejoy?"

The brushwork was perfect. He'd even got a good original frame, just that wrong screaming yellow.

"Lovejoy? I asked if you're married." I dragged my eyes away.

"Do I look it?"

She tilted her head, smiling, finally said no.

"I suppose my frayed drip-dry shirt gave me away."

She laughed at that. I was beginning to like her but shook the feeling off. No dawdling allowed in the antique game, Lovejoy. When times are especially bad, physical love—and everything else—comes a long second. Lovejoy Antiques, Inc., were fighting for survival, and this in a trade where Genghis Khan wouldn't last a week.

"You have an eye for style," I flattered, still concentrating on the picture.

"A present to Peter, my husband. It isn't actually old at all. A friend did it, poor old Mr. Bexon. Isn't it good?"

"Great." I went to sit close beside her, suddenly very bleak. *Poor old* Mr. Bexon? I didn't like the sound of that. Poor's okay and old's okay, but *poor old* sounds a goner.

"It's very similar to the Castle's paintings, isn't it?" the dear little innocent said.

"Very similar," I agreed. Just how similar she would probably never realize. I avoided telling her anything about it, though.

The reason people are bitter about us dealers is that they believe us to be openly on the make (true) and unerringly skillful at recognizing genuine antiques (on the whole, hopelessly wrong. Most of us couldn't tell a Ch'ien Lung vase from a jam jar under a laser beam. I'm an exception.)

"Divorced?"

"Eh?"

"I said are you divorced?" Brenda repeated.

"Yes. Her name was Cissie." Best to be honest when they are

4

doing their intuition thing. "It was my fault, really." It had been like living with Torquemada.

She nodded, but women don't really agree with this sort of manly admission. Shrewd to the last, they *know* everything's always the woman's fault. I just go along with the majority view.

"Too wrapped up in art," I explained. "It was just after I'd joined Christie's."

"Sotheby's," she corrected. I'd given her the wrong card. She'd actually read it, the pest. I wish women were more reliable.

"Ah," I said, quick as a flash, "I was with both of them at that time. Spreading the genius around," I added, smiling to show I was still modest deep down. "Is Mr. Bexon a neighbor?" Poverty makes you very single-minded.

"He lived here in the village. So wonderful with children." Oh dear, that past tense.

"Was?" I managed to get out.

"He died a few weeks ago. Of course he was very old." People annoy me saying that. Is death not supposed to count just because you're getting on? She put her arms around me and moved closer. "It was fantastic with you, Lovejoy."

"Yes, great," I said, now thoroughly depressed. Another empty.

"I don't . . . you know, for every man who comes knocking."

"No, love." They always go through this.

"You're special."

"Did he work with your husband?"

"With Peter? Yes, once. Engineering."

I shrugged and gave in. We were just becoming active again when she said these precious words which ruined all chance of really closer acquaintance.

"I'm glad you liked the painting. If Peter hadn't called to collect it one weekend it would have gone with the rest of his things in the sale."

"*Sale?*" I dragged my hands from her blouse and withdrew swiftly along the sofa, fumbling for my shoes.

"Why, yes."

"Where?" I broke into a sweat. "Quick. *Where?*"

"In town. That auction place, Gimbert's. What's the matter, Lovejoy?"

"When?"

"Good gracious!" she exclaimed. "You look as if you've seen a—"

"*When?*"

"Last week." She couldn't miss the chance of criticizing another woman. "There was some...bother. So I heard. His nieces had a terrible row. Nichole's quite nice but Kate—"

"Was there much stuff?" I snapped, but saw her pout and had to slow up. "I have to ask, love, or I get in trouble," I said, desperate. "You do understand."

"It's all right," she said bravely. "It was really quite pitiful. I happened to be, well, passing when the van arrived. It was so sad. He only had a few old things."

It was so bloody sad all right. A few pitiful *old things*? Belonging to an old genius who could forge Restoration with such class? Moaning softly I was off the sofa like a selling-plater.

"Goodness!" I yelped over my shoulder. "Look at the time!"

She trotted dolefully after me toward the door. "Do you have to go? Will you come again, Lovejoy?" she said.

"Yes, yes! Thursday. Is a town bus due?" I babbled.

"Not for two hours. Better Monday," she cried. "Safer on Monday. Peter's golfing then. Like today."

"Right, Brenda. See you Monday."

"I'm Mary," she said, all hurt.

"Mary, then." I could have sworn she'd said Brenda.

I was out of the street and running in a sweat through the village toward the main road. Women are born quibblers. Ever noticed that?

2

Nothing on the main road. Never a bus when you want one. We used to have Nathan's Fliers, three crackpot single deckers which ran fast and on time between the villages, operated by a corrupt old lecher called Nathan. Then we were amalgamated with the nearby big towns, and all buses have become either late or extinct. I stood there, cursing.

I tried thumbing a couple of cars but no luck. That's the trouble with East Anglia, too much countryside. Nothing but undulating countryside, mile after mile of rivers, lush fields and woods dotted with small villages. Merrie England. I sometimes feel as if Lovejoy Antiques, Inc.'s the only outfit keeping this particular bit Merrie, especially after a week on the knocker. When I'm reduced to going on the sound (that's banging at doors and asking if people have anything old for sale, the surest sign of impending failure in the antique business) I stick to towns if I can. Countryside gives me the willies. Everything in it seems to eat everything else, preferably alive. It can get you down.

You'll have guessed I'm a real townie. As things get worse, though, you have to go farther afield. Villages are best for antiques. They're antique themselves. So there I was in Great Hawkam, two villages from home. Stuck. Bexon's forgery the only good link I'd had for months and no chance for a lift. The situation called for desperate remedies. The pub beckoned.

I knew it a little, the Goat and Compasses, built in King Stephen's reign while his mob were scrapping with the volatile and exotic Empress Matilda. Paid for, I shouldn't wonder, in those ugly hammered silver coins of his—now so rare and prized it's no good even dreaming about them. I sprinted over. Maybe I'd get one in my change.

I entered briskly, hoping to create an impression of a dealer who had just come from doing a deal for everything the National Gallery wanted this year. A dozen or so people were destressing from the village's hectic social whirl, including Lennie. He's Victoriana, bygones, glass, crystalware and clueless. I swiftly borrowed a coin off him, partly because I had no change and partly because it's cheaper. I rushed through to the phone and dialed like a maniac.

"Hello?" I put my voice on. "Is that Mrs. Markham's residence?"

"Yes. Who is it, please?"

"This is Doctor Chenies of the hospital," I said, sounding really good. "Could I speak to Mrs. Markham? It's urgent. About her friend, Mrs. Witherspoon."

"Oh, right." He sounded suspicious. People who don't trust people get me really mad. Why is there no trust these days? Where has it all gone?

"Hello, Doctor?" Janie's voice, thank God. "I'm afraid you must have the wrong—"

"It's me. Lovejoy." I heard her stifle a laugh. "Come and get me."

"Is it really urgent, Doctor?" she said, doing her hesitant friend act. "My husband has guests—"

"Stuff his guests," I snarled. "I'm stuck out in the bloody wilds here. The pub at Great Hawkham crossroads. I'm in a hurry."

"Very well, Doctor. I'll try to come—"

"Be sharp." I slammed the blower down. I honestly don't know what women think they're playing at sometimes. Full of wrong priorities.

I readjusted my face to a casual smile and strolled back to the saloon bar where Lennie waited. I told him about a wonderful deal I'd just made, buying a Georgian embroidery frame and an early Sheffie. He was all ears and plunged further into his natural gloom. Not that there's such a thing as really very early Sheffield plate. The term's relative. It was only invented in the 1740s by Thomas Bolsover (please don't spell his name with a "u" stuck in there—he hated it). Elkington finished off the boom in fused sheets of copper and silver by inventing electroplating in 1840.

My eyes wandered while Lennie grumbled on about some Caffieri cast bronzes he'd missed. Dottie Quant was on a bar stool, straining half a mile of stylish leg to reach the ground and making sure we all noticed. She's ceramics and silver, in the local antique arcade. Her legs bring in a lot of deals, they say. I believe it. I waved over, nodding affably, and got a sneer in return. That's better than my average. Distaste from Dottie's like a knighthood. She was talking to a fairhaired thickset man, maybe a stray golfer or a buyer? Her balding husband grovelled about trying to coax his noonday sneer from his alluring wife. A domestic rural scene.

I promised to sell Lennie my mythical embroidery frame. I offered to buy him a drink, and escaped before he could draw breath and say yes please. I blew Dottie a noisy kiss to get her mad and left, my mind dazzled by old Bexon's wonderful faked painting which might mean so much.

*

What messes people get themselves in, I was thinking as I crossed the road. I stood waiting for Janie under the trees for coolth. There's Lennie, in his wealthy mother-in-law's clutches more ways than somewhat. And there's Dottie having to rub at least shoulders with the riffraff, and her with carriage trade aspirations and a whining hubby.

Still, I'd my own problems. Where the hell could I locate a late Georgian embroidery frame by Saturday? The problem was worsened by not having any money to buy, even if I found one.

A week ago I'd missed a rosewood table—you won't believe this—actually signed by Timothy Walford, about 1810, complete with fringed base-edge carving on triple scrolls. If this page is wet it's because I'm sobbing. Good class furniture with a provincial maker's name is so rare. It was sold an hour before I reached the Arcade. What with taxes and an unbelievably greedy public life's hard.

You may be developing a low opinion of my most endearing qualities. Don't. My qualities are yours, folks. I would have been as fascinated and excited by old Bexon's lovely forgery if I'd just made a million in gold minutes before, instead of being broke and getting desperate. I tell you all this now because the behavior you actually see around antiques is only the tip of the dealer's iceberg. From there it sinks on and on, down and down to include the thousands of fearsome emotions sociologists do not know. And if at the end of this you think I'm lascivious, crude, sexist and selfish, do you know anybody who isn't?

Janie drew up, calling gaily, "Hello, sailor!" Her joke.

"Where've you been?" I said coldly. "I've been here an hour."

"I've been exactly ten minutes," she said, calmly eyeing me. I climbed into her Lagonda. "Where've you been?"

"Working." And how hard, I thought.

"You look exhausted, Lovejoy."

"I am."

"Was she worth it?" she asked sweetly, pulling out.

"If you're going to nag—"

"And where were you last night?"

"Ah," I said, thinking quickly. "I got stuck."

"In . . . ?" she prompted, all bright innocence.

"Cut it out, Janie." I tried to seem annoyed. "With a deal."

"Anything really good?"

"No." True, true.

"Where are we going?"

"Woody's."

"That filthy place gives me fleas, Lovejoy."

"It gives me a living. Or rather," I added bitterly, "it should do."

"Let me, Lovejoy." A pause while hedges and fields swished by. "Give you a living," she added.

I turned to watch her drive. The Lagonda didn't even purr. Janie's beautiful, twenty-six, wealthy in her own right. Her husband's wealthy too. He often goes abroad to mend companies

sick of the palsy. Crackpot. They have a mansion in Little Hawkham, smaller by two houses than Great Hawkham, the one I'd
just been working.

"I'm good value," she said, smiling. "Worth a quid or two.
Good legs. Teeth my own. Socially trained, convent-educated. I
could buy an antiques auction firm for you to play with. Think,
Lovejoy. And take your hand off my knee when I'm driving."

"And your husband?"

"Who?" She gave me a 1920 stare, trying to make me laugh.
They only do that when they're serious. "Spell it."

"Look, love," I said wearily. "Am I loyal?" You can't muck
about. You have to tell them outright.

"No."

"Kind?"

"Never."

"Considerate?"

"Hopeless."

I went down the list of virtues getting a denial every time.

"Then what's the use?"

"You're worth it, Lovejoy," she said after a think. "You understand what love is. If only you weren't an escapist."

"Flight has a long tradition of success," I got back. She
wouldn't let go, though.

"Besides," she said, "something's always happening around
you."

"I wish it bloody well was," I groused.

Now I wish I hadn't said that. Not that I'm superstitious, but
you can't be sure, can you?

3

Janie dropped me at the corner post office among prams and shoppers. I told her twenty minutes. Woody's Bar tries to hide itself in an alley between a pub and a jeweler's but gives itself away by gushing out steamy blue fumes, swamping the pavement. Wise pedestrians cross over. The alley's partly covered, and is known as the Arcade to locals. It looks like a beginner's cardboard cut-out Camelot joined together wrong. Bloody town council planners. The beauty is that it's crammed with antique dealers' shops.

I pushed into Woody's Bar and peered through the opaque air. There he was. Tinker Dill, my barker, among the crammed tables. He was lashing into one of Woody's specials and hastily trying to sober up before the pubs got under way again. It's not a pretty sight. A dozen other dealers were about, wolfing mounds of chips, sausages and mashed triffid greasily concealed under slithering mounds of ketchup. I tell you this trade needs nerve.

"Tea, Woody," I called into the blue haze toward the back. He'd be there, smoking ash into some poor soul's charring haddock.

"Hello, Lovejoy," a few voices called. I waved, a picture of the successful antique dealer. Cheerful adversity is vaguely entertaining, but even friends steer clear of doom.

I sat and watched Tinker Dill eat. All this yap about civilization really is utter cock. Civilization isn't art, religion and all

12

that. It's two things: paving and cutlery. Without paving everything's jungle. Without cutlery eating's a clumsy dissection
which ends by stuffing pieces of dead animals and plants between your jaws. Tinker does it without a net.

"Tinker."

No reply.

"Tinker," I tried again, louder. Not a sign. "Money," I said
softly. The place stilled with utter reverence. At the magic word
even Woody's clattering pans had silenced.

I watched Tinker begin to respond to therapy. I've known him
years but it's still gruesome. Bloodshot eyes swiveled as if
searching for the next planet. Stubble, corrugated black teeth,
skeletal limbs shuffled into human shape. He's thin as a lath.
His lazaroid knuckles are always concealed under ketchup-
stained woollen mittens, his frame lost somewhere in an overcoat straight from the Crimea.

Tinker's brain fidgeted painfully into action. His eyes focused,
two raw balls wobbling in gin-soaked aspic. He saw me.

"Hello, Lovejoy."

"Did you pin the scrambler?" I asked.

"Yeh." He was coming around.

"Settle later, okay?"

"Yeh." (Translation: Tinker Dill reports he has successfully
found a Georgian hurdy-gurdy for me, complete with animated
French figurines. He would get it, and I'd pay him enough commission to get sloshed out of his mind again.) To continue:

"Great," I praised.

Tinker crumpled a grin. The tension all about eased and noise
began again. Woody's giant waitress Lisa loomed in the fog with
my tea like the *Bismarck* through its last smokescreen.

"How's Lovejoy?" She ruffled my thatch.

"Poor. Lonely." Disbelieving snickers rose from nearby tables.
"No money, but good company." She surged away, smiling.

"You're always after crumpet, Lovejoy," Tinker criticized piously. He goes to chapel, but I hear the wine's free.

I waited while he shoveled his huge meal away like a smelter
frantically raising steam. All around muttered deals were being
made, messages muttered through mouthfuls of grease and tea
just too weak to plow. The door tinkled. A tourist peered briefly

in and reeled away at the sight of huddled, feeding, smoking, belching humanity still stinking of last night's booze.

To me Woody's permanent fry-up is like a church, holy, something to venerate. Blasphemy? Come down one day and see for yourself. There'll be a Woody's in your town, full of antique collectors and dealers. If you stick it for more than two days you'll be hooked for life on antiques because there's no denying that sense of religious devotion. Antiques are everything, even the reason for living. Nothing else exists. It's the feeling that makes crusades. I know because I have it, have had it for years. Dealers are dealers down to the marrow and out to the skin again, no variation or treachery. And more money passes across Woody's unwashed grease-smeared tables in one week than our town councillors fiddle in a whole year, and that's enough to refloat the franc. Woody's is beautiful.

"Better, Tinker?"

"Yeh." Tinker finished elegantly as ever, settling like a tattered combine harvester coming to rest. He wiped his mouth on a stained mitten and emitted three rhythmic belches. I got Lisa to bring him a pint of tea. He lit a cigarette, in paradise. Hangover gone, smoking, tea in hand, having survived Woody's breakfast, the auction coming up tomorrow, pulling off a find and almost sober enough to start getting stoned again. To business.

"Bexon," I began. "Old bloke, died. Some stuff got into Gimbert's auction last week."

"What was it?"

"I don't know."

"Hang on."

He slurped from his cup to fuel up for cerebral activity. His eyes hazed. I swear his brain becomes audible. He took a deep drag of carcinogens. Blast off.

"Bexon. An old geezer? Great Hawkham?" he remembered finally. I nodded. "Only rubbish."

"No paintings?"

"None. Rough old furniture, ordinary modern junk. Couple of carpets."

"Find out about Bexon, Tinker." My heart was in my boots.

"Is it urgent, Lovejoy?"

14

"You just don't know." I gave him one of my stares and he nodded. It's his job to be concerned about whatever I'm concerned about. It's more than his job—it's his life. Barkers are scouts for antique dealers, the foragers, the pilot fishes questing ahead of the predatory shark . . . er, sorry, that last metaphor's unfortunate. Skirmishers, perhaps. "And try for a Georgian embroidery frame, Tinker." A few quid from Lennie wouldn't come amiss.

"Very hard, Lovejoy."

"Nothing from the robbery up for sale?" I asked helplessly, really scraping the barrel.

Yobbos had hit our Castle museum a couple of weeks before, nicked some ancient British-Roman gold coins and used most of them in slot machines for cigarettes. This is akin to using a Kakeimon bowl for afters or clicking a La Chaumette flintlock from curiosity. The intellects our local lads have. Hopeless. If you stood them outside St. Paul's Cathedral they'd see nothing but a big stone bubble. I'm not being cruel. Most can't tell a gold-mounted glass Vachette snuffbox from a box of aspirins. I mean it. The only gold-and-glass snuffbox ever discovered in our town made by that brilliant Napoleonic goldsmith was being used for aspirins at some old dear's bedside. Two years ago a marine barometer made with delicacy and love by André-Charles Boule of Louis XIV fame was cheerfully nailed in place to span a gap in a shelf in a local farm cottage.

You just have no idea. East Anglia drives you mad sometimes. It's paradise to a good, honest dealer like me, but I thank heavens da Vinci wasn't local. His silly old scribbles would have been used for wallpaper in a flash.

"No."

"Any news of the coins?" He shook his head.

About three of the tiny—but oh, so precious—gold coins were still missing, according to the papers. Of course, I was only interested because I wanted to see them returned to their rightful community ownership in the museum for future generations to enjoy. Nothing was further from my mind than hoping they'd turn up by chance so a poor vigilant dealer like me could snaffle them and gloat over those delicious precious ancient gold disks positively glinting with . . . er, sorry. I get carried away.

15

"Hang on, Lovejoy."

I paused in the act of rising to go. Tinker was quite literally steaming. The pong was indescribable, stale beer and no washing, but he's the best barker in the business. I respect his legwork if nothing else. And he stays loyal, even with things this bad. I let him fester a moment more, looking about.

Helen was in, a surprise. She should have been viewing for tomorrow's auction this late in the day. One of our careful dealers, Helen is tall, reserved, hooked on fairings, Oriental art and African ethnology. I'd been a friend of Helen's when she arrived four years before, without ever having felt close to her—mentally, that is. Self-made and self-preserved. She usually eats yogurts and crusts in her sterile home near our ruined abbey, St. John's. Odd to see her in Woody's grime.

"Slumming?" I called over cheerily to pass the time. She turned cool blue eyes on me, and breathed cigarette smoke with effect like they can.

"Yes," she said evenly and went back to stirring coffee amid a chorus of chuckles. Lovejoy silenced.

"Lovejoy." Tinker Dill was back from outer space. "What sort of stuff did you want from Bexon?"

"Paintings."

He thought and his face cleared.

"Dandy Jack."

"He picked up something of Bexon's?" I kept my voice down. Friends may be friends, but dealers are listeners.

"Yeh. A little drawing and some dross."

"Where is he?" Dandy's shop was across the main street.

"On a pick-up."

Just my luck. Dandy was given to these sudden magpie jaunts around the country. He always returned loaded with crud, but occasionally fetched the odd desirable home.

"Back tomorrow," Tinker added.

"On to something, Lovejoy?" Beck's voice, next table. Beck's a florid flabby predator from Cornwall. We call his sort of dealers trawlies, perhaps after trawler-fishing. They go wherever tourists flock, usually one step ahead of the main drove. You make your precarious living as a trawlie by guessing the tourists' mood. For example, if you can guess that this year's east coast

16

visitors will go berserk over pottery souvenirs, plastic gnomes or fancy hats you can make a fortune. If you guess wrong you don't. A rough game. Beck fancies himself as an antique trawlie. I don't like him, mainly because he doesn't care what he handles—or how. He always seems to be sneering. A criminal in search of a crime. We've had a few brushes in the past.

"Is that you, Beck, old pal?" I asked delightedly into the fumes of Woody's frying cholesterol.

"Who's Bexon?" he growled across at us.

"Naughty old eavesdropping Big-Ears," I said playfully. Not that I was feeling particularly chirpy, but happiness gets his sort down.

"Chop the deal with me, Lovejoy?" To chop is to share. There's nothing more offensive than a trawlie trying to wheedle.

"Perhaps on another occasion," I declined politely. I could see he was getting mad. The dealers around us were beginning to take an interest in our light social banter. You know the way friends do.

"Make it soon," he said. "I hear you're bust."

"Tell the Chancellor," I got back. "Maybe he'll cut my tax."

"Put that in your begging bowl." He flicked a penny onto our table as he rose to go. There was general hilarity at my expense.

"Thanks, Beck." I put it in my jacket pocket. "You can give me the rest later." A few laughs on my side.

We all watched him go. Local dealers don't care for trawlies. They tend to arrive in a "circus," as we call it, a small group viciously bent on rapid and extortionate profit. They're galling enough to make you mix metaphors. Take my tip: never buy antiques from a travelling dealer. And if there are two or more dealers on the hoof together, then especially don't.

"Watch Beck, Lovejoy," Tinker warned in an undertone. "A right lad. His circus'll be around all month."

"Find me Dandy Jack, Tinker."

"Right." He wheezed stale beer fumes at me.

I rose, giddy. A few other dealers emitted the odd parting jeer. I waved to my public and slid out. I was well into the Arcade before I realized I'd forgotten to pay Lisa for my tea. Tut-tut. Still, you can't think of everything.

As I emerged Janie signalled at me from near the post office, tapping her watch helplessly. Duty obviously called. I must have been longer than I thought. Through the traffic I signalled okay, I'd stay. I'd phone later. She signalled back not before seven. I signalled eight, then. I watched her go, and crossed back to the Arcade. Now I'd drawn a blank over Bexon, poverty weighed me down. I meant to go but you can't avoid just looking at antiques, can you? Especially not in the Arcade. Patrick yoo-hooed me over to his place before I'd gone a few windows. I forced my way across the stream of people. He always embarrasses me. Not because he's, well, odd, but because he shows off and everybody stares.

"Just the little *mannikin* I've prayed for!" he screeched, false eyelashes and fingers all aflutter. "Lovejoy! Come here this very instant!" Heads were turning and people gaped at the apparition posturing in his shop doorway. "This way, Lovejoy, dearie!" he trilled. I was a yard away by then.

"Shut your row, Patrick." I entered the shop's dusk. "And must you wear a blue frock?"

"Ultramarine, you great buffoon!" he snapped. "Everybody pay attention!" He did a pivot and pointed at me in tableau. "Lovejoy's in one of his moods." The trouble is I always go red and shuffle. I can only think of cutting remarks on the way home.

"Don't mind Patrick, Lovejoy." I might have known Lily would be there. I don't have time to tell you everything that goes on, but Lily (married) loves and desires Patrick (single and bent). Lily insists—in the long tradition of women hooked on sacrificial martyrdom—that she's just the bird to straighten Patrick. As if that's not enough, both are antique dealers. You see the problem. "He tried to get a museum expert over," Lily explained, "but he's gone to Norfolk." She spoke as if Norfolk were in Ursa Major. Our locals are very clannish.

"This way, dear heart!" Patrick sailed to the rear followed by the adoring Lily. Three or four customers hastily got out of the way of someone so obviously and flamboyantly an expert as Patrick. I trailed along. *"Regardez!"*

It was a stoneware bottle. A large fish swam lazily in brushed iron design under the celadon glaze. I reached out reverently, chest tight and breath dry. My mind was clanging with greed and love as I turned the little table around to see better.

"Pick it up, Lovejoy," Patrick offered.

"Shut up."

"Oh!" he snapped petulantly. "Isn't he absolutely *vulgar*."

I sat and let the beauty wash from the brilliant work of art into the shop. The master had coated the bottle's body with a luscious white slip. It was lovely, a lovely miracle. The ninth-century Korean pots are very different—those imprinted with hundreds of those tiny whorled designs in vertical rows tend to get me down a bit. This was from a much later period.

"It's genuine, Patrick," I said brokenly. "Superb."

"You perfect *dear*, Lovejoy!" he whooped ecstatically.

"Korean, about latish fifteenth century."

Excited, he dragged me away and showed me a few other items—a phony Meissen, a modern Hong Kong copy of a Persian-influenced Russian silver gilt tea and coffee service, supposedly 1840 (it's surprising, but modern Eastern copies always give themselves away by too rigid a design) and suchlike. We had a final row about a William and Mary commemorative plate. He was furious, wanting everything he showed me to be genuine now.

"It's a genuine blue-and-yellow, Lovejoy!" he protested.

"I'm sure it is, Lovejoy." That from the anxious Lily, unbiased as ever.

"It's modern," I said. I touched it. Not a single beat of life in the poor thing. "They always get the weight and colors wrong. The yellow should be mustard. The blue should be very blue." The dazzling loveliness of that Korean bottle was making me irritable. I added, "You know, Patrick. Blue. Like your frock."

He wailed into tears at that. I left, feeling poorer than ever and a swine. For all I knew ultramarine might have been his color.

*

Still two hours to wait for a bus home. And still all blank. I strolled toward the Castle museum. It was time I saw what sort of antique coins had been stolen, in case.

The town museum is in the Castle. Its new curator's a small tidy man called Popplewell. I got to him by telling a succession of uniformed opponents I wanted to make a donation to the museum. One even tried to charge me admission, the cheek of it. People take my breath away sometimes.

"Donation?" I told Popplewell, puzzled at the mistake. "I'm afraid one of your assistants got it wrong. I said nothing about any donations. I'm here about the robbery."

"Ah," he said dismally. "Insurance?"

Now, to digress one split second. Insurance and I—and I strongly urge this to include you as well—do not mix. As far as antiques are concerned, forget insurance. Concentrate what money you have on the antique's protection in the first place. Don't go throwing good money away.

"No," I said, rapidly going off him. "I'm an antique dealer."

"Really," he said in that drawl which means, I've met your sort before.

"I want to know what was nicked in case it gets offered me."

"Is that so?" He eyed me suspiciously, reclassifying me as a lout.

"Yes. They'll start looking for a fence," I explained. "They may take the goods to one of us respectable dealers."

"I see." He came to a decision. "Very well. I'll show you. This way please."

I didn't tell him Lovejoy's Law for the detection of stolen antiques, which runs: any genuine antique offered to you at a third of its known price has been stolen. Blokes like this curator chap are just out of this world. You need somebody like me to amass a collection, not a dozen committees.

We puffed on to the Roman landing. Popplewell halted at a sloping case. He removed a board and its covering beige cloth. The glass beneath was shattered and the display cards all awry. The legend card read, "Gold Coins of the Roman Period: Britain." Popplewell took my stricken expression for criticism.

"We haven't had time to establish a substitute display," he said. "And the police have taken scrapings and photos for prints."

"Could you be more specific about the items?"

"A set of Roman staters. Gold. Claudius, And some silver." He saw me reading the cards scattered in the case. It had been a rough smash-and-grab. "Those are Mr. Bexon's own labels."

"Er, Bexon?" I sounded hoarse all of a sudden.

"Top right hand corner." He pointed. "The donor wanted his own labels retained. Quite incorrect, of course, but . . ." he shrugged.

I read them through the broken glass, careful not to touch because police can be very funny about fingerprints. The cards all said the same: "Gold coins, Roman period." Then a curious sentence on each: "Found by the donor, Roman Province of IOM." I read this aloud.

"Was he serious? Isle of Man? But the Romans—"

Popplewell shrugged again. "I believe he was a somewhat eccentric old gentleman. He insisted that we adhere to that wording exactly, though we all know that the Isle of Man never was colonized." He covered the scene of the crime. "We have the most amazing conditions appended to our gifts sometimes. I could tell you—"

"Thank you," I interrupted hastily. "One thing. Were they genuine?"

"Of course." He got nasty. "If you mean to imply this museum doesn't examine properly and in detail all—"

"Er, fine, fine," I said, and moved off. "If I hear anything I'll let you know."

"Good. You have the phone number?"

The Castle galleries run three sides of the square, leaving a huge central well crowded with visitors at this time of year. Helen saw me looking and waved upward quite calmly from where she was inspecting one of the coaches on display there. I waved back. Helen wasn't thinking of going in for Queen Anne coaches, that was for sure. When I'd climbed down she'd gone.

I walked thoughtfully across the drawbridge among tourists and children, and found I was worried sick. Bexon isn't all that common a name. I decided to look in at Margaret's. I still had time before the bus.

Hers is the only shop with a good dose of sunshine. She looked up and came limping to welcome me with a smile. I'm too fond of Margaret. There's a husband somewhere in the background but I've never had the courage to ask, though I do know she has a good range of some man's suitings in her bedroom wardrobe. We know each other fairly well. I like Margaret more than I ought, but you get days, don't you. I slouched in like a refugee.

"Stop that," I told her irritably.

Margaret was twisting a pewter burette. On a good day it turns my stomach. You can imagine what it does to me on a bad one.

"Hello, Lovejoy," she hesitated. "I'm seeing if it's genuine."

"Trust its appearance," I growled. "Why torture it just because you're ignorant?"

"Charming," she said, but she had no right to get nettled.

Dealers get me sometimes. We're all as bad. Pewter's the most maligned, crippled and assaulted of all antiques. Dealers who reckon to show they know a thing or two twist pewter, actually grab hold and twist it hard. When you do it hard enough it screams, screams from its poor little soul. Well, wouldn't you? Really tears you apart. It's a terrible, wailing scream like a child in intractable pain. Only pewter does it. Dealers, the bums, think it's clever. People do similar sorts of things to jade. Ignorant collectors say that if you can scratch it with a key it isn't genuine, which is rubbish. Any reasonable jewelers will give you (free) a card showing Mohs' Scale of hardness for semiprecious stones, which tells you all you need to know about what can scratch what. There's no excuse for simple ignorance. Never be cruel to antiques, folks. They've done nothing to you, so don't go about massacring them. And pewter's got a fascinating history. Of course, it can be very difficult to collect though you can still buy good pre-Conquest specimens. It was actually forbidden in churches at the Council of Westminster after A.D. 1175, but the French allowed it by their Council of Nîmes, 1252, so there's plenty around, and eventually our lot saw the light again. More sense in those days.

I took the little wine vessel from Margaret. It looked like the mark of Richard Marbor, 1706—a yeoman and therefore fairly well recorded. Good old Henry VIII took a little time off from attending to Anne of Cleaves in 1540 to encourage the York pewterers to record their touch-marks on their wares, so a lot is known. I told her all this, and added that there's no reason to go throttling these delicate antiques when you can learn twice as much by reading and just looking.

"Tea?" Margaret offered by way of thanks.

"Er, no, thanks." Margaret's tea's a legend among survivors. "Who's best with Roman coins around here, besides Cooney?"

Cooney's a mad half-Spanish dog-breeder who lives down on the marshes. He's been divorced six times and he's only twenty-eight.

"There's him," she said, "and Pilsen. And that magistrate." She counted on her fingers. "And that overcoat man."

We have a few eccentrics hereabouts. The man with the overcoats is a local living legend. Like Charles Peace, he's rumored to have a fatal attraction for women, which of course may just be him boxing clever, it being well known that women are oddly attracted by such stories. He collects overcoats and Stuart coins. The magistrate is an elderly man who fought at Jutland or somewhere. He's hammered Edward I silver coins. Pilsen's a dealer with a one-room lock-up shop on the Lexton village road. He makes kites and has religion.

"Thanks, love." I rose to go.

"Lovejoy." Here it came. I'd watched her working up to it inch by inch. "What's it about? You aren't usually uneasy."

"I'm not uneasy," I said.

"Anything I can do?"

"Look. If I wanted to find out how somebody died," I asked, taking the plunge, "how would I go about it?"

"The doctor, I suppose. But he won't tell unless you're the next of kin."

"What about Somerset House?"

"Better the local registration office. That's nearer."

I gave her a kiss and departed.

The woman at the registration office was helpful. Poor old Bexon's death certificate showed he'd passed away without causing the slightest bother or suspicion. Nothing out of the ordinary to hold up wills or bequests. She was pleased at how tidy everything was.

I stood at the bus stop thinking so hard I almost forgot to get on when it finally came.

4

I live in this cottage, often alone, on the edge of a village a few miles from our main town. There's a garden, a copse, blackthorn hedges good for purple sloe gin at Michaelmas, and a muddy path I keep meaning to macadam over. The village lane begins at my gate. Further down there's just a path to the river's shallow watersplash at Fordleigh. I always set my break-in alarm because we dealers are forever being burgled. It has to be flicked before unlocking the door or Police Constable Geoffrey, our village Sherlock, gets hauled out of his tomato-ridden greenhouse to pedal over and tell me off again for causing false alarms.

Once in the cottage I was at a loose end. I just couldn't get going. Everybody has a blue patch now and then, I suppose. I'm normally a buoyant sort, but I couldn't settle down to anything. It rained an hour or two about four, so I washed this week's socks and swept up. The vacuum was on the blink so I did without. The village's one shop had pasties in. I got two for supper and some tomatoes.

Normally I read over a meal. This evening I found myself staring at the same page, reading a paragraph of Dean Inge's essays over and over. Poor old Bexon kept coming into my mind. A forger, but apparently an honest one. Why else that revealing yellow? So he was honest, the poor innocent. But those Roman

golds. Popplewell said they were genuine. The labels said mostly Nero's reign. There were even one or two showing the babes
being suckled by the wild she-wolf, Romulus and Remus.
Rome's originals. And the famous arched "DE BRITANN" gold
of Claudius the God. Well, all right, but there never was such a
thing as a Roman province of the Isle of Man. Everybody knows
that. They simply never got there. Even if they heard of it they'd
ignored it.

A wrong label's the sort of odd mistake you pass off in any
museum. A million like it happen every day. But the picture in
Mary's house was done with love and almost incredible skill.
And gold's gold. And, far more to the point, a Roman antique's a
Roman antique. I thought on, guiltily knowing I should have
been bringing my notes up to date.

At the finish I gave up and got a map. You can see why they
didn't occupy it, of course, way out in the middle of the Irish
Sea. Not wealthy, not very populous, probably poor weather
much of the year. No wonder. I locked the front door, drew the
curtains and rolled back the living-room carpet.

The easy way to lift the giant flagstone would have been to
use a beam winch rigged to a two-horsepower motor connected
to the iron ring set in the floor. That would have been a bit obvious, though, so I lift it with my own lilywhites. There's a switch
by the steps leading down into the priest-hole. Nothing had
been disturbed. It was probably an old vegetable store, but
you'll have noticed by now I'm incurably romantic, if a bit cyni-
cal with it. There are a few tea chests down there for storing my
vast stock of priceless antiques (temporarily sold to buy a luxury
called food). It's ideal for storing antiques. The old folk had their
heads screwed on. Nowadays it's all builders can do to stick
houses down straight, let alone include anything useful for the
occupants.

I drew out the folding Regency table and opened my card in-
dex. Antiques impose their own demand on any dealer worth a
light, penniless or not. I meet it by keeping notes. Paper clip-
pings, book abstracts, catalogued details from sales, hints picked
up at auctions, eavesdroppings, museum listings—many horribly
wrong, by the way—and advertisements, all get stored away. I

searched frantically for any suggestion of a brilliant forger oper-
ating locally. Plenty of duds, and one or two not so bad. But brilliant? Not a sign. I looked up names.

I found two Bexons. One's a collector in Norwich. He's
hooked on Victorian mechanicals. Three years before he tri-
umphed by snapping up a beautiful late model of Thomas New-
comen's engine. He must be still paying, but I'd bet he was smiling through his tears. Mechanicals are worth their weight in
gold, plus ten per cent, of course. The second Bexon was a regu-
lar buyer of *découpage*—paper cutouts varnished onto surfaces
for decoration of furniture, ornaments, firescreens, tableware
and such. In itself it's a small antique field, but you can say the
same about Leonardo da Vinci's stuff, can't you?

More worried than ever that I'd somehow missed a really
golden opportunity, I closed up.

I went out to check my two budgerigars as soon as it stopped
raining. The garden was drenched, the grass squelching under-
foot. A sea wind had sprung up. As darkness falls my cottage
seems to move silently away from the two other houses nearby.
One had lights in the window tonight. I was pleased about this
though it was only old Mrs. Tewson and her dog. I checked the
budgies' flight with a torch and said goodnight. They fluffed and
chirped.

The budgerigars, Manton and Wilkinson, were how I'd met
Janie. I'd done over one of the stallholders on our Saturday market. He'd had the birds in an old shoe box covered by a piece of
glass, no food or water. Practically accidentally, I'd stumbled
against him, breaking his shoulder, poor man, after buying them
from him. Worse, I'd accidentally broken his fingers by standing
on his hand. The police had come along and tried to make a case
out of it, but luckily Janie saw it all and explained it was an accident. They'd let me go suspiciously, which only goes to show
how they're completely lacking in trust these days. I'd taken one
look at Janie, smiling and wealthy, and that was that. She'd giv-
en me a lift back, helped me to buy the cage and seed, and matters took their own course, as folks say. Janie says I'm soft about
them, but I'm not. At the moment I could only think of Bexon.
Forger or not, he was my lifeline back into the antique business.

Inside the cottage I fidgeted and then cleared up and fidgeted again. I even wished I hadn't had to pawn the telly. Isn't it funny how you get feelings. I decided to use my one remaining asset and phone the names Margaret'd given me. Cooney's always in because of his dog kennels. I told him I was interested in the stolen coins.

"You and the rest of us, Lovejoy," he said, laughing.

"From the Isle of Man," I explained innocently. He snorted disbelievingly.

"There's no such thing," he told me. "Oh, they've had the odd stray Roman denarius show up, but no hoards or anything like that. The old chap who donated them went about saying he'd found them there."

"Where?"

"On Man. Wouldn't say exactly. There was a row about the labels, I remember. He insisted on writing his own."

"Thanks, Cooney."

I got Pilsen next, the only religious antique dealer-cum-kite-collector in the universe. He blessed me down the phone and intoned a short prayer for my success but couldn't help. He tried to sell me a kite but forgave me when I said some other time. The old magistrate barked that the robbers should be horse-whipped and slammed the receiver down when I admitted I had no Edward I coinage for sale. The overcoat man after a chat gave me a commission to bid for him at a local auction for an officer's greatcoat of the Essex Regiment, but otherwise nothing.

No use phoning Janie when I had the blues, though she'd be blazing tomorrow. You can't help being on edge sometimes.

Imagine suddenly meeting somebody who believed they could prove there'd been a hitherto unidentified king of England whose existence nobody else had ever suspected. Or an extra American president. Or an extra moon for Earth. I felt just like that.

It probably didn't matter, I decided. The wrongest guess I ever made.

I decided to sleep on it but tossed and turned all night.

5

Next morning Janie was waiting, illegally parked, pretending to look at the cutler's wares in Head Street. I'd caught her by phone just as she was going out for a hairdo. We agreed to make up over coffee. She took one look at my face.

"Oh, dear."

We went to a place near Gimbert's auction rooms on East Hill. I could see them unloading the antique furniture from the window table. Janie paid, pretending to do it absent-mindedly so I wouldn't take it bad.

I told her the tale of Patrick's wonderful find, the Korean vase. She said I should have tried to learn where he'd got it, but that's something dealers never do. She listened about Bexon, Popplewell, the Roman golds. I told her that Dandy Jack had got hold of the remnants of old Bexon's belongings.

"What's the mystery?"

"There never was a Roman province of the Isle of Man, Janie. Caesar never bothered."

"Then where did the coins come from?"

"Exactly." I stirred uncomfortably. The nasty feeling was still there. Earlier I'd found Mary's surname from the register and telephoned. Her husband had been golfing since dawn, obviously a nutter. "Take me to the golf club, Janie."

"My God, Lovejoy! How can I?" She shook her head. "My

neighbor's a golfer. I'd better drop you beyond the station bridge. Can I come round later if I can get away?"

"No," I said too quickly. "Er, I've a deal on." I do a special job at home some afternoons which Janie doesn't know about. Tell you about it in a minute.

"If I find you haven't, Lovejoy," she said sweetly, "I'll murder you. I hope you understand that."

"Don't start," I pleaded, but she put her lips thin the way they do and wouldn't answer. Women never trust people. Ever noticed that? Sometimes I wish they would. It'd make my arrangements so much easier.

Janie ran me to the railway, periodically telling me to take my hand off her knee when she was driving, but it was honestly accidental. It's a mile uphill from the station bridge. The golf club stands back from the narrow road among trees, quite a fetching low building. You never pass it without seeing a score of cars.

I asked for Peter Chape in the bar. He was out on the course. I waited, watching golfers from the bar window. I have no interest. To me golf's a good walk spoiled. Behind me people entered the bar, had a drink, smoked. I listened to the talk of birdies, eagles, five irons and rough chipping. It was another language to me, like Swahili. The great thing, it seems, is to ask everybody else what their handicap is. Mine's women.

I was being pointed out to a tall newcomer by the barman. He started across the room. Peter, Mary's husband.

Peter Chape was a thin, rather casual man, disappointed that I wasn't a golfer. I explained I was a dealer searching for Bexon's paintings and told innocently how I had been directed to his house earlier in the week by some anonymous well-wisher. He confirmed what Mary had said about old Mr. Bexon. They worked as engineers together only for a short period before the old chap retired.

"He lived with his two girls," he said. "Nieces by adoption, really. Kept house and so on. A quiet, clever old chap."

"I believe they're easy to get along with," I fished cleverly. "Maybe I should call around."

"Well . . . Nichole, yes. Katie . . . maybe not so easy." Clearly the gentlemanly sort. I thanked him and went.

It's a long walk out to the village. Not one antique shop for ten miles in any direction. A short cut runs across fields into our village but I never take it. There's too much countryside about already without going looking for the rotten stuff. As I walked I kept wondering if mashie niblick was in the dictionary.

*

It was coming on to rain as I trudged eventually into my lane. A familiar motorcycle was propped against the cottage. I groaned. I'd forgotten Algernon, a trainee would-be dealer lumbered on me by a kindly crucifixioneer. I was struggling to educate him in antiques. Talk about a sow's ear.

It was becoming one of those days again.

"Lovejoy!" He was coming round the garden, beaming at me through his goggles. Toothy, specs, motorcycle leathers. He's mad on bikes.

"Hiyer, Algernon. You'll frighten the budgies in that gear."

"I've read it." He dragged from among his leathers a book and held it up, proud as a peacock. "Like you said."

"Not in the rain, Algernon." I took the precious volume and put it inside my jacket.

"Fascinating! Such an amazing group of people!"

I squinted at him. The burke was serious. If I ever strangled him I'd have to get Janie for an alibi. He was wagging like a gleeful dog fetching its stick.

"An absolutely marvellous read," he was saying when his voice cut out. That was on account of my hand scrunging his windpipe. I pinned him against the wall.

"*Goon!*"

He was puce. I took my hand away and watched the cyanosis go.

"But, Lovejoy!" he gasped. "What's wrong?"

Algernon is a typical member of the public. That is to say, piteously ignorant of practically everything, but mainly and most painful of all entirely ignorant of antiques. Trying to teach a twenty-two-year-old Neanderthal the trade was the result of my habit of going broke. Algernon was steadily breaking my heart.

"What book," I asked gently, "did I give you?"

30

Algernon backed away. He was beginning to realize all was not well.

"*Biographical Memoirs of Extraordinary Painters.*"

"By?"

"William Beckford. Seventeen eighty."

"And you took it seriously?" I yelled.

"B—b—but you said study it." He fell over his bike, backing off.

I leaned over him. They say Beckett put his face to the wall when asked about his plays. Sometimes I know exactly how he felt.

"Algernon," I said. "Beckford's showing us the stupidity of the fashionable artistic judgment of his times." I watched light dawn in his thin, spotty countenance. "Are you receiving me, Algernon?"

"I *see!* A literary joke!" He scrambed to his feet, all excited. "How clever!" I just don't believe in people like Algernon. I've stood him next to a Turner oil and he's not even trembled in ecstasy. "I'll read it again!" he exclaimed. "I will keep that new satirical aspect uppermost in mind!" He really talks like this, the Piltdowner. No wonder he's thick.

"Tomorrow, Algernon," I said slowly, carefully not battering his brain to pulp, "you come here—"

"Thank you, Lovejoy! I accept your kind invitation—"

I struggled to keep control, my voice level gravel. "By tomorrow make sure you've read Wills on Victorian glass and Baines on brass instruments."

"But tomorrow's only a day away," he said brightly.

"It always is, Algernon," I cut in. "But it's still the deadline. And you'll get your next test on miscellaneous antiques."

"Yes, Lovejoy." His face fell. He hates tests. I gave him the Beckford again and stood in the porch to wave him off. He fired his bike and boomed away, waving and grinning through the hedge's thin bits.

"You're too hard on Algernon," Janie's always saying, but she's wrong. I just worry about him. As a dealer Algernon wouldn't last a month. Where I come from he'd starve. I switched the alarm key and went in.

I made some soup from one of those crinkly packets, three sandwiches—fish paste and tomato—and brewed up. No sugar in case it made me feel guilty. I had one egg left which I was saving because Henry was due at teatime. He's ten months old and my second visible means of support. Henry's the special job I mentioned earlier. Well, it's not my fault.

*

When you're broke a number of quite interesting things happen. You see at first a whole new set of people you otherwise would have missed: milkmen, children, housewives, shopkeepers. You get to recognize bus conductors because you've no car. Cyclists come and ride talkatively alongside as you bike into town. The second thing's that old demon gelt—one clink and you prick up your ears like a warhorse at a bugle. The money problem intrudes. It gets everywhere, like soot. Everything reminds you of it—women, the garden, posting a letter, wondering if you can afford a newspaper. You become a sort of accountant. It's really rather unpleasing. The third thing is that people start agreeing with what you say and even with what you think. It's very odd. Like if you buy a lettuce and you're thinking, that's a hell of a lot of money just for one measly lettuce. Ten to one a horde of other shoppers will be at your elbow in a flash, all saying, "It is a lot, love. For one lettuce! Isn't it terrible?" and things like that. The point is, nobody would have said a thing before you got broke. See what I mean?

I'd been destitute some three weeks before the local village housewives understood. Gradually they began pausing at the gate if they were down my lane. We started exchanging the odd word in our one street. It was pretty pleasant. There are even hidden fringe benefits but I'd better not go into that, because people gossip so. I kept up a front for a week or two ("Well, I've a lot of work to do at home, so I've not gone in today . . .") but it was only politeness. They realized. After that I found myself winkled into their problems, women being born winklers. Before long I was going errands into town for medicines and then doing the shopping for them. From there I was walking dogs and holding keys to let the oil people deliver. They paid me in change, odd tips. My final graduation in social acceptance was Henry.

I asked Eleanor—his mother, twenty-five, wife of a publisher—what to do with him but got no straight answers. She said Henry eats most things, by which she meant everything, including light furniture and curtains. He never seems to do much, just lies about and mutters. Once you actually get to know him he's a ball of fire. At first I was worried when it was his hometime because Eleanor never used to check him over. I wanted to show her he wasn't at death's dark door on return of goods, even thinking of making her sign a receipt in case he was sick in the night and I got blamed. He lasted out the first week, though, and after that I stopped bothering. I was daft to worry because Henry's as hard as nails. Eleanor gives me tips for helping her, a quid here and there. I know it's not very dignified, in case that's what you're thinking, but it keeps me in the antique game during these bad patches. That's what matters.

I finished my grub, chucked the remains to the robin and thought about the old genius with his two ratty nieces. I was getting a permanent feeling about it, but maybe it was the fish paste.

*

I've got to tell you about Henry's revolting habits here, because without them I'd never have got any further with the Bexon problem. In fact, in a way Henry lit on my first clue.

Eleanor came racing up the lane five minutes early, out of breath as usual. Henry was strapped in his push-chair, jerking as she ran.

"I'm late, Lovejoy!" she gasped. She always says this. "Hurry!"

"I don't have to," I pointed out. "I'm staying here. It's you that's going somewhere."

"And I'm late! Goodbye, Henry darling. Be good!" We go through this rigmarole every time, saying the same things. I don't mind, though it's unproductive.

She streaks off to collect her two children from our village school, which is why I lodge Henry.

I wheeled Henry in and unfixed him. He got ready to laugh. We have this joke. I opened his coat and peered.

"Nope. Still no hairs on your chest yet, Henry," I said sadly. He roared at that, his favorite and most hilarious quip. He was still falling about when I carried him to the divan. They never look heavy, do they? Henry's a crippling welterweight.

"Let's see what she's put in for you today, Sunbeam." I opened his bag. It comes fastened on his pram thing. We looked at his teatime offering distastefully. "Fancy it?" A tin of baby food, a really neffie powdery stuff. We'd tried it a couple of times at first but I think I made it wrong. He went off it after one spoonful. Two rusks and a little tin of some tarry stuff were the rest of his ration, which he eyed with hatred. You can't blame him because his food looks so utterly boring. "Then there's nothing for it, Cisco," I told him. "Chips, sardines and . . . an egg!" I held it up to excited applause.

I carry Henry about while I make his tea. It's not easy. Women have hips and can simply hold spherical offspring on their ledge. They've also got the fascinating knack of somehow walking slanted. Men, being basically cylindrical, have no ledge to speak of. It's tough, needing continuous muscular effort. I natter about my day's work while I get going.

"Another list of dazzling failures, Henry," I told him. "No luck. But I saw a picture. . ." I explained what a clever forgery Bexon had made. "Some old geezer from Great Hawkham." Henry watched me open the tin of sardines, a drool of saliva bouncing from his chin. "What do you reckon?" He said nothing, just pistoned his legs and ogled the grub. "If I'd done a lovely forgery job like that I'd have found some swine like Beck and sold it to him."

Henry chuckled, clearly pleased at the idea of doing a trawlie like Beck in the eye. Maybe he had an antique dealer's chromosomes surging about in his little marrow. I peeled two spuds and hotted the oil.

"Instead," I went on, "he paints in a wrong color. Giveaway. And don't try telling me—" I shook the peeler at Henry warningly—"that it was a simple mistake. It was deliberate." Saying it straight out made it seem even weirder. I gave him the whole tale. At least Henry listens. Algernon's not got half his sense. "The more you think about it, Henry," I said seriously, "the odder it becomes. Odderer and odderer. Right?"

I put him down and gave him a ruler to chew while I fried up. I told him about the golds. He tends to follow you around the room with his eyes. I leave the kitchen alcove uncurtained while I cook so I can keep an eye on my one and only ruler. They're expensive.

I was prattling on, saying how I was hoping to pick up the rest of Bexon's stuff from Dandy Jack, when the bell rang. It's an old puller, 1814. (Incidentally, household wrought ironwork of even late Victorian vintage is one of the few kinds of desirables you can still afford. It's becoming a serious collectors' field. Decorative industrial ironwork will be the next most sought-after. Don't say I haven't warned you.) I wiped my hands and went into the hall. Janie's silhouette at the frosted glass. Great. All I needed.

I rushed about hiding Henry's stuff and cursing under my breath. The bloody push-chair wouldn't fold so I dragged it into the main room and rammed it behind a curtain.

"This is all your fault," I hissed at Henry. He was rolling in the aisles again, thinking it another game. "Look." I pushed my fist threateningly at his face. "One sound out of you, that's all. Just one sound." It didn't do much good. He was convulsed, cackling and kicking. I told him bitterly he was no help but anything I say only sends him off into belly laughs. He never believes I'm serious. Nothing else for it. I went to the door.

"Hello, love." My casual Lovejoy-at-ease image. A mild but pleased surprise lit my countenance at seeing Janie again so soon.

"You've been an age answering." Janie gave me a kiss and tried to push past. I stood my ground. She halted, her smile dying. "What's the matter, Lovejoy?"

"Matter? Nothing," I said, debonair. I leant casually on the doorjamb all ready for a friendly chat.

Her eyes hardened. "Have I called at the wrong time?" There was that sugary voice again.

"Er, no. Of course not."

She stared stonily over my shoulder. "Who've you got in there, Lovejoy?"

"In—?" I managed a gay lighthearted chuckle. "Why, nobody. What on earth makes you think—?"

"I go to all this trouble to get this box of rubbish from that filthy old man," she blazed, "and all the time you're—"

"Jack?" I yelped. "Dandy Jack?"

"You horrid—"

"You found Dandy?" She was carrying an old cardboard shoe box. I took it reverently and carried it into the hall. I didn't notice Janie storm past.

I removed the lid carefully. There was the inevitable jamjar full of old buttons—Why the hell do people store buttons? Everybody's at it—a rusty tin of assorted campaign medals, expression of an entire nation's undying gratitude for four years of shelling in blood-soaked trenches, and a loose pack of old photographs held together by a rubber band. At the bottom were two worn but modern exercise books, cheap and pathetic. It really did look rubbish as Tinker Dill said. My heart plunged.

"Is that all, Janie?"

She was standing in the hall behind me, desperately trying to hold back a smile.

"I trust," she said with pretended iciness, "you've some perfectly reasonable explanation for your little friend in there?"

"I asked if this is everything," I said sharply. Now she'd rumbled Henry it had to be first things first.

"There's a sketch," she said. "Dandy wouldn't sell it me. What's he called?"

"What did it look like?" I led her into the room. She picked Henry up to fawn on him. He gazed dispassionately back, probably wondering if the changed arrangements meant less grub all around.

"He wouldn't show me."

I put the box down dejectedly. Disappointments come in waves. While I went back to doing Henry's tea she told me how she'd phoned Tinker Dill at the White Hart. He'd found where Dandy Jack was by then, somewhere over Ipswich way. She'd scooted along the main A-12 coast road and cornered Dandy at a little antique fair—the sort I had the money to go to. Once.

"I thought you'd got some woman in here," she said.

"I see." I went all hurt, obviously cut to the quick at such mistrust.

"Don't be offended, Lovejoy." She came over and put her arms around me. "I know I shouldn't be so suspicious."

One up, I relented and explained about Henry. She thought he was delightful but was up in arms about his food.

"You're not giving him *that!*"

"What's wrong with it?" It looked all right to me. I poured the sardine oil on the egg to save waste.

"I thought it was yours, Lovejoy!"

"I've had mine." I shook sauce on. Henry was all on the go.

"Dear God!" she exclaimed faintly. "Does his mother know?"

"Well, actually," I confessed, "I chuck his powder away so she won't worry." In fact I sometimes eat it to fill odd corners. Well, Henry's a gannet. I can't afford to feed us both properly and his own food tastes horrible. He's not so dumb.

Janie watched in horror as I fed him. All this mystique about feeding babies is rubbish. It's not difficult. You prop them up in some convenient spot and push bits toward their mouth. It opens. Slide it in lengthwise but remember to snatch your fingers back for further use. The inside looks soft and gummy but it works like a car cruncher. You have to concentrate. I mean, for example, it's not the sort of thing you can do while reading.

"His face gets some too," I told her.

"So I noticed." She looked stunned.

"It's all right. There's no waste. I scrape it off and put it in afterwards. It's his big finish."

"My God. I feel ill."

I was rather put out by Janie's reaction. Secretly I'd expected her to be full of admiration at my domestic skills. Admittedly he was beginning to get a bit smudged but that always happens. "Try it. You can tell when he's finished," I added. "He starts spitting out."

"What a mess. How does the poor little mite survive, Lovejoy?"

37

I ignored this. No meal's ever pretty, is it?

"Mind your manners." Women are great critics, mainly when they see other people doing all right. It's mostly jealousy. "I think he's full." He was bulging but still moving impatiently. "Time for pudding."

"There's *more*?"

I'd got Henry two pieces of nougat, which would have to do for today's afters. I was embarrassed, Janie being there to see it wasn't done as properly as it should be. Puddings should be on a plate and everything with custard.

"Here. Unwrap it." She took the nougat carefully. "Hold it by one end and push a corner in his mouth," I told her. "Blot the dribbles as you go."

Once she got going I took Bexon's pathetic belongings and began to rummage.

"Dandy said he'd give you the sketch if you'd scan for him," Janie said, intent on Henry.

We were all sprawled on the divan.

"Dandy would," I said bitterly. Scanning means examining supposed antiques to separate genuine items from the junk. I hate doing it for others. It's something I never do normally, only when I'm broke. Dealers are always on at me to scan for them because I'm a divvie.

"Where does this infant put it all, for heaven's sake?" Janie exclaimed. She glanced across and saw I was flicking through one of the exercise books. "You're wasting your time with that rubbish. I've looked."

"Keep your mind on your job," I said. I hate being interrupted.

It *was* rubbish. The old exercise books were just scribbled boredom, perhaps some fragments of a diary of the sort one always means to start but never quite gets around to. Dejected, I decided on the spur of the moment to teach Henry to read, which of course made Janie split her sides. I've tried before but Henry ate the highly educational alphabetic book I got him. I showed him a line and said to concentrate. He seemed to be amused, but obligingly gaped at the pages while he noshed the nougat.

"I then caught the train back to Groundle Glen," I intoned, pointing to the words as I read.

"They start learning on single letters, Lovejoy," Janie criticized.

I reached for the other booklet. Maybe there was a set of capitals.

"I then caught the train back ... " caught my eye. "Hello. What have we here?" It was the ninth page about halfway down. "That's the same sentence."

I flipped through the pages in the first notebook. The sentence was identical, ninth page about halfway down.

"What is it, Lovejoy?"

"They say the same things." And they did, both dog-eared exercise books. "One's a copy of the other."

The pages were ruled, obviously for school use. About twelve pages were filled with meticulous writing, ballpoint. I examined both books swiftly. The texts were identical, word by word. Even the blot on page ten was carefully copied into the other book's tenth page. Each written sheet was signed "James R. Bexon." I picked a page at random. Page six. The other book's page six was identical, sentence for sentence, down to the last comma. Crazy.

"If you ask me he's a madman," Janie said. "Who writes a diary, then copies it out all over again?"

Maybe the old man *was* a maniac. The Restoration forgery and its clever giveaway leapt into my mind. Then again, I thought carefully, maybe he wasn't.

"Bexon was no nutter. I've seen a painting he did." I checked Henry over. "He'll need changing in a few minutes."

While Henry whittled his way through the rest of his nougat I read one of Bexon's exercise books. Absent replies from me kept Janie going while she prattled away, how she'd buy a town house for us and I could keep the cottage on if I really wished. I was absorbed.

*

The diary was twelve pages, each page one day. A simple, sentimental old chap's account of how he had a holiday on the

Isle of Man. The dates were those of a couple of years previously. It was all pretty dreary stuff. Well, almost all.

He'd rented a bungalow, walked about, visited places he'd known once years before. He'd gone to the cinema and hadn't thought much of it. Pub on a few occasions at night. He complained about prices. Chats with taxi drivers, boats arriving and the harbor scenes. He'd gone about, seen a few Viking tumuli and Celtic-British remains, watched the sea, ridden on an excursion. Television shows, weather. It was dead average and inordinately dull. Home on the Liverpool ferryboat. Argument with a man over a suitcase. Train to London, then bus out to Great Hawkham. That was it.

But there was this odd paragraph about the coffin. The same in both books, in Bexon's careful handwriting:

> I eventually decided to leave them all in the lead coffin, exactly where I would remember best. I can't face the publicity at my age— TV interviewers are such barbarians. That is to say, some three hundred yards from where I first dug down on to the mosaic terracing. I may give a mixed few to the Castle. Let the blighters guess.

Both diaries continued with chitchat, how the streets of Douglas had altered after all these years and what changes Millicent would have noticed. That was his wife. Apparently they'd honeymooned on the Isle years before.

"It sounds so normal there," Janie said into my ear. "Even sensible." She'd been reading over my shoulder. Careless old Lovejoy.

"Very normal," I agreed. Then why did it feel so odd?

"What do you think he gave to the Castle?" she asked. Henry gave a flutelike belch about C-sharp.

"Heaven knows," I said as casually as possible. Popplewell's face floated back. The cracked glass, the cards in disarray under the cloth. "It could have been anything. Henry needs changing. The clean nappy's in his sponge-bag."

I half-filled a plastic bucket with water and undid him. It's easy as long as you stick to the routine. Unpin him on a newspaper, wash off what you can in the lavatory, chuck the dirty nappy in the bucket and wash him in a bowl. Then dry and dust. Five minutes.

"Eleanor takes the dirty one," I explained.

I set about making some coffee. I keep meaning to buy filter-papers and a pot thing but so far I've never managed to get beyond that instant stuff.

"Lovejoy. Mine's different after all." She'd been showing Henry how the pages turned. "At the back."

I came over.

"There's a drawing of a lady in mine. Yours hasn't."

On the inside cover Bexon—or somebody—had painstakingly drawn a snotty crinolined lady riding in a crazy one-wheeled carriage, splashing mud and water as it went. A carriage with one wheel? It looked mad, quite crazy. The drawing was entitled "Lady Isabella." Pencil, Bexon's hand.

"There's no horse pulling it," Janie pointed out. "And only one wheel, silly old man."

"Unless . . . Janie." I fetched coffee over. Henry likes his strong. "You said Dandy Jack has a separate sketch?"

"Yes. He said he'll see you tomorrow."

We all thought hard.

"So if there's a message," I reasoned aloud, "it's in the words, not the sketch. The drawing's only a guide."

"Oh, Lovejoy!" This made her collapse laughing. "You're like a child! Are you sure it isn't a coded message from the Black Hand Gang?"

"Cut that out," I said coldly, but she was helpless laughing.

"Anyway, who in their right minds would make a coffin out of lead?" she gasped.

"You're right." I gave in sheepishly and we were friends again.

But the Romans did.

                    *

You know, sometimes events gang up on you. Even if you decide against doing a thing, circumstances can force you to do it in the end. Ever had that sensation? The last time I'd had the same feeling somebody'd got themselves killed and the blood had splashed on me. For the rest of Henry's time we played on the divan. I'd invented this game where I make my hands into hollow shapes and Henry tries to find the way in.

41

I shivered. Janie looked at me a bit oddly. She switched the fire on, saying it was getting chilly. Henry began to snore, about an octave deeper than his belches.

"He sleeps for an hour now, till Eleanor comes," I said. "You'd better go just before she calls." I didn't want my women customers believing the cottage was a den of vice.

I lay back and watched the ceiling.

*

I've been assuming up to now you know the facts, but maybe I'd better slip them in here. If you're a bag of nerves you should skip this bit. It gives me nightmares even yet, and I read it first as a lad at school.

Once upon a time our peaceful old land was still and quiet. All was tranquil. Farmers farmed. Cattle hung about the way they do. Folk didn't fight much. Fields, little towns, neat forests and houses, Thursday markets. Your actual average peace. Then one day an anchor splashed in the Medway, to the surprise of all.

The Romans had landed.

The legions, with Claudius the God Emperor bored stiff on his best war elephant, paraded down our High Street after dusting over the Trinovantes, boss tribe in those days. Our town was called Colonia, capital of the new colony of Britain under Governor-General Suetonius.

It would have all gone smoothly, if only the Druids had not got up his Roman nose. They skulked over to Anglesey, off the coast of Wales, almost as if Rome could be ignored. Well, you can imagine. Suetonius was peeved and set off after them, leaving (here it comes) Britain in the hands of tax gatherers. Usual, but unwise, because Claudius was a real big spender and had left millions for the tribal kings as a gesture of goodwill. The politicians showed up and pinched the money. Sound familiar? They had a ball—especially the night they raped the daughters of a certain lady called Boadicea.

Now Boadicea was no local barmaid. She happened to be Queen of the Iceni, a tough mob. Breasts seethed in the Iceni kingdom. And, remember, Suetonius was away in Anglesey with his legions, a detail the arrogant conquerors forgot.

It was all suddenly too much for the bewildered British tribes. One dark day the terrible Iceni rose. The whole of Eastern England smoldered as the Roman settlements were annihilated crunch by savage crunch. The famous Ninth Legion strolled out from Lincoln, innocently intending to chastize the local rabble, a shovel to stop an avalanche. The thousands of legionaries died in a macabre lunatic battle in the dank forests. St. Albans was obliterated in a single evening's holocaust. The outposts and the river stations were snuffed as Boadicea's grim blue-painted hordes churned southward, until only the brand new Roman city of Colonia was left. Catus the Procurator skipped to Gaul in a flash, promising legions which never came. Politicians.

There was nothing left but the smoldering forests, the waiting city and silence. Then the spooks began. The statue of Victory tumbling to the ground and swivelling its sightless stone eyes ominously away from Rome. Omens multiplied. Rivers ran red. Air burned. Statues wailed in temples. I won't go on if you don't mind. You get the picture.

Finally, one gruesome dark wet dawn Boadicea's warmen erupted from the forests, coming at a low fast run in their tens of thousands. The Temple of Jupiter, with the Roman populace crammed inside, was burned. The rest were slaughtered in the streets. The city was razed. Boadicea jauntily crucified seventy thousand people, Roman and Briton alike, and nobody survived. It's called patriotism.

In the nick of time Suetonius miraculously returned to evacuate London, shoving everybody south of the Thames while Boadicea burned London and everywhere else she could think of. See what I mean, about women never giving up. Naturally, Rome being Rome, Suetonius made a comeback and the British queen took poison after her great defeat, woman to the last.

I'd always accepted the story at its face value, but now I couldn't help wondering about something which had never struck me before.

Hadn't Suetonius been a long time coming back?

*

Nowadays our locals say to newcomers, "Don't dig below the ash, will you? The ash is so good for the roses. And there's bits of

43

bone, too. Calcium and phosphorus. We're quite famous for our roses hereabouts." It's such good advice to gardeners.

I don't do any gardening.

*

Janie went in the nick of time. Eleanor collected Henry, now awake and singing with his foot in his mouth. I'm really proud of that trick, but Janie said they all do it. I waved from the front door.

I cleared up and got the map. The Isle of Anglesey is about half a mile from the Welsh coast. Thomas Telford even flung a bridge over the narrow Menai Straits. (Incidentally, Telford's engraved designs are worth far more nowadays than the paper they're printed on. They're hardly impressionistic but give me first choice of any you get.) One old historian, Polydore Vergil, always said Suetonius invaded the Isle of Man but he was an erratic Italian everybody said was a nut anyway. There is even a belief that Suetonius had with him the famous Gemini Legion, but that must be wrong as well.

Augustus Caesar once received a delegation from a far country and is reputed to have whispered behind his hand to an aide: "Are they worth conquering?" The country happened to be Ceylon, Sri Lanka, which for size could dwarf Rome any day of the week. The point is that the ancient Romans were distinctly cool. And one of the coolest was Suetonius, that dour, unsmiling, decisive and superb soldier whose tactical judgment, however grim, was unswervingly accurate.

As the evening drew on I tried to light a fire but the bloody wood was wet. I switched on the electric again instead. The birds outside had shut up. Only the robin was left on a low apple branch. My hedgehogs were milling about for nothing, rolling from side to side like fat brown shoppers.

Had the might of Rome been paralyzed by a stretch of water you can spit over? Was Suetonius held up by a few Druids booing on the other side? History says yes. This old chap Bexon was telling me no.

I gazed at the garden till it was too dark to see.

44

6

Next morning I shaved before seven. I had some cereal in powdered milk and fed the robin my last bit of cheese. I went to have a word with Manton and Wilkinson, gave them their groundsel.

"Now, Manton," I demanded as it noshed its greenery sitting on my arm, "what's all this Roman jazz?"

It wisely said nothing, knowing there was more to come.

"The old man leaves two diaries. But why two?"

Wilkinson flew on me for his share.

"If he was crackers, let's forget it, eh?" They hesitated suspiciously. "On the other hand, curators may be duck eggs but Popplewell can tell genuine Roman antiques, coins or otherwise. Right?" They closed up along my arm, interested now. "Bexon's coins being genuine, pals, what can there possibly be, I wonder, stuck in an old lead coffin in some well-remembered spot in the Isle of Man?"

We thought hard.

"And who should benefit better," I demanded, "than Lovejoy Antiques, Inc.?"

Wilkinson fluffed out, pleased. Manton looked sceptical.

"Don't be so bloody miserable," I told Manton angrily, "just because I haven't the fare to get there. You're always critical."

I shoved them onto a branch and shut their flight door. Both were looking sceptical now.

"I can get some money," I snapped. "Don't you worry. I'll have the sketch *and* the fare from Dandy. I'll be back. You'll see."

By my front door the robin was cackling with fury. He was quite full but battling to keep the sparrows from the cheese he didn't want. Very feminine, robins.

The bus was on time. In my innocence I thought it a good omen.

*

Dandy Jack's is a typical lock-up, a shop front and two rooms. The clutter held miscellaneous modern tarted up as old, a brass 1890 bedstead (worth more than you'd think, incidentally), pottery, wooden furniture and some ornamentals plus a small gaggle of portabilia in a glass-fronted cabinet.

A few people milled about inside, mostly grockles (dealers' slang: tourists, not necessarily foreign, derogatory) and the odd dealer. Big Frank Wilson from Suffolk was there. He gave me a nod which said, nothing worth a groat. I shrugged. He's Regency silver by desire, William IV furniture by obligation, and undetected bigamist by the skin of his teeth, as if scratching a quid in the antique game isn't enough nightmare to be going on with. Jenny from the coast (she's tapestries and Georgian household items) was painstakingly examining a crate of porcelain. She and Harry Bateman were desperately trying to stock up their new shop on East Hill. They'd badly overspent lately to catch the tourist wave, but their stuff was too "thin" (dealers' slang again: much low quality spiced with only rare desirable items).

I pushed among the driftwood—not being unkind, but I really had seen better antiques on Mersea beach.

"Hello, Lovejoy."

"What's new, Dandy?"

"Bloody near everything," he grinned. I had to laugh. "Message for you from Bill Fairdale. He says to call in."

Bill was from my village, rare manuscripts and antique musical instruments. The only trouble was that his rare illuminated manuscripts are a bit too good to be true. The sheepskin parchments pegged out drying in his garden do very little to restore a buyer's confidence. He's even been known to ask a visitor's help in mixing "medieval" monks' egg-tempera pigments with an unfinished carpet page of Lindisfarne design in clear view, only to offer the same visitor the completed "antique" next day. He's very forgetful.

"Has his handwriting improved any?"

Dandy Jack fell about at my merry quip. Once, Bill actually acquired a genuine love-letter from Horatio to his dearest Emma Hamilton. Nobody else dared believe Bill. I bought it for a song. That's the danger of forging too much and not doing it well enough. A happy memory.

"He's got something right up your street."

It was probably that bone flute, cased, sold in Bury the previous week. I'd heard Bill had gone up. Potter, the great old London maker, if Tinker was right. Very desirable. I said nothing, nodding that I'd pop in.

"I want a favor, Dandy. A certain sketch."

His eyes gleamed. "Come back here." We withdrew into his inner sanctum. He offered to brew up but my stomach turned. That left him free to slosh out a gill of gin. Dandy was permanently kaylied. He perched on a stool opposite his crammed sink, shoddy and cheerful, a very rum mixture. Where I think in terms of mark-up, Dandy thinks booze. I've never seen him sober in n years, where n is a very large finite integer. He has a good eye, sadly wasted.

"An old chap called Bexon. You got his stuff at Gimbert's auction."

"Your young lady spoke to me yesterday. I gave her the box."

"That's only rubbish, but he was an old friend and—"

"Yeah, yeah," he said. "Never mind all that, Lovejoy."

I said, desperate now, "She said you had a sketch he did."

"That sketch'll cost you."

"How much?"

"Do me a scan and you can have it free."

"Get lost," I groaned. It always came down to this, from fellow dealers too useless to do their own work.

"Go on, Lovejoy. You're a divvie. Help me out." I had enough trouble without feeling sympathy.

"Commission?" I tried hopelessly but the wretch was grinning. He knew he had me and shook his head.

"Scan my stuff or you don't even get to see Bexon's picture."

"All right," I gave in bitterly. "Anyhow, your commission wouldn't keep me in pobs."

"My stuff's in that crate. I'll fetch it."

He dragged in a tea chest of miscellaneous porcelain, followed by Jenny Bateman protesting she'd not finished looking.

"Hard luck," Dandy told her, pushing her out. All heart.

"Is this it?" I hate scanning junk.

"A job lot. There's a ton of valuable stuff in there, Lovejoy." The eternal cry of mankind since Adam dressed.

I sat wearily, waiting for the mystic mood to come over my mind. A divvie always suffers. Having friends irritates me sometimes. I closed my eyes and stilled. Sounds receded. The world slipped into silence and all feeling fell gradually into the distance.

*

Divvie? Maybe from the old word "diviner," as in water, but who knows? It's slang for anybody who can guess right about a thing without actually knowing. Some people have it for gems or paintings, others for racehorses, thoroughbred dogs or scenic design, a precious knack that goes separate from any learning. I'm an antique divvie. And, incidentally, I'm the very best there is.

I've tried asking other divvies how they know, what actually happens. Some say they are "told," others say it's a feeling. Water diviners say it's a foot-tingle or a twisting stick. To me it's a kind of bell, and it rings in my chest. My knowledge, on the other hand, only tells me what an antique is. But my bell just rings for truth. And look, folks—good news. *Everybody* alive has this knack for *some* thing. Maybe not for antiques or diamonds, but for *some* thing. Nobody's been left out. It's superb news really, because you're included, too. You. All you need to find is what your particular gift is for. You might actually be the most original and creative porcelain or furniture expert without knowing it. If you don't already know you're being dreadfully wasted.

The way I do it is to get as close as possible, look and then maybe a light touch if that's not damaging to the antique. Always remember to leave antiques alone. Never fondle, clean, wipe, polish or brush. And I don't mean "hardly ever," like in the song. Never is never. Leave antiques alone. Never scrape, improve, smooth, fill in or dissect. Remember that all antiques really are Goya, Chippendale, Sheraton or Michelangelo until proved otherwise. If you say that yours aren't, I'd like to know what makes you so sure.

Dandy Jack was very considerate as I worked, tiptoeing in like a steamhammer for another pint of White Horse and having a hell of a row with a customer over the price of a modern vase he swore was Ming. Honestly, my head was throbbing by the time I finished. I was famished.

"Dandy," I called. "Done." He dropped a pile of books with a crash and reeled in.

"Prime stuff, eh, Lovejoy?"

"Not bad."

He grinned at the three objects on the table and nodded wisely.

"Bloody rubbish," he agreed. "I knew it was all valuable except for them."

"They're the good stuff, Dandy." I rose, stretching. "Chuck the rest."

"Eh?" He glared into the heaped chest. "All this? Duff?"

"Duff," I nodded. "Have you any grub?"

"Margaret fetched these over for you. She'll call back." He held out a brown paper bag toward me, two whist pies and an eccles cake.

I sat and ate, recovering, while I explained the three pieces to him. He listened, quite mystified.

"Candle snuffer, Worcester." I nodded at the smallest item, a tiny bust of a hooded Victorian woman. "It's 1864, give or take a year." I hate them. Collectors don't.

"Pity it's not earlier." He peered blearily in my direction. Good old Dandy. Always wrong, not even just usually.

There was a shaving mug shaped like a white monkey, grotesque with an exquisite glaze. I honestly don't know what the Victorians were thinking about, some of the things they made.

49

The bowl was the precious item, though Dandy Jack could see nothing special about it. Like I say, some people can hear fish squeak. Others wouldn't hear a train in a tunnel. He said it looked like Spode, when it was clear Daniel, early 1830s. I tried not to stare at the lovely thing, but the elevated tooled bird motifs in gold, with curves resting on feet of bright blossoms, dragged my eyes. Blues screamed at pinks, greens and shimmering maroons in a cascade of color. It sounds garish, but it really is class, and incredibly underpriced at today's prices, though that only means for a second or two. Dandy was more than a little narked that the rest was mostly junk.

"Bexon's sketch, Dandy," I reminded him. Scanning stuff really takes it out of me, why I don't know. After all, it's only sitting and looking.

"Here."

I took the drawing from Dandy's grimy hands. Bong went my chest. Simple, stylish, very real, a tiny pencil caricature with some color. It was her again. The artist had pencilled her name in, Lady Isabella. She was the same snooty lass, doubtless made to look starchier than in real life, riding in a high absurd one-wheeled carriage with idiotically long shafts and no horse. The wheel splashed water as it rolled through the streets. It was probably one of those crazy skits they got very worked up about before steam radio and television blunted pens and sense.

"Is that all?"

"Yes. Straight up, Lovejoy. What is it?"

"Looks like a caricature. Genuine Burne-Jones."

"Genuine?" A long pause, during which Greed crept ominously in. "I'll give you the rubbish for nothing, Lovejoy," Dandy said. Oh-ho, I thought. Here we go.

"You said—"

He crouched into his whining position. "Look, Lovejoy—"

"Bastard." I should have known he'd let me down, though Dandy Jack's no worse than the rest of us.

"No, honestly, Lovejoy. I didn't mean I'd give you the drawing as well."

"Sure, sure," I said bitterly. I was unable to resist one final glance at the Burne-Jones. He was a Victorian painter, a bit of a lad who did a few dozen caricatures to amuse Maria Zambaco, a gorgeous Greek bird he shacked up with for three years. Maybe Maria put him up to sketching one of her bosom friends.

Dandy offered me a drink but I staggered out into the oxygen layer, as broke as when I'd arrived. That's typical of some days in this trade.

There was a blue Lagonda occupying two-thirds of the High Street.

"At last, Lovejoy."

"Oh. Hello." I really was pleased to see her. It's the way it gets.

"Well?" She nodded at Dandy Jack's window. "Did you get the picture?"

"Er, no," I said lamely. "He, er, he wanted to hang on to it—"

"You mean he won't give it to you?" she fired back. She stepped out angrily. "You look drained. Have you scanned for him?"

"Yes, but—"

"Right. Wait here." I caught hold of her.

"No, love. I'm not up to a battle today—"

"You're a *fool*, Lovejoy," she stormed. "No wonder you're penniless. You let everybody take advantage—"

I turned away, meaning to walk off because people were beginning to stare. And this lovely blonde was standing beside me, breathless and pretty.

"Excuse me, please," she said. A picture, her lovely face anxious and her deep eyes troubled. "Are you Lovejoy? Can I have a word, please?" There she stood, nice, worried, determined. Her smile was brilliant, full of allure. Women really have it. I decided I needn't walk off after all.

"Yes, dear?" Janie cooed. She drummed her fingers on her elbows, smiling.

Now, women don't like each other. Ever noticed that? If two meet, you can see them both instantly thinking (a) what's this bitch *really* up to? (b) thank God her clothes are a mess, and, following on pretty smartly, (c) isn't it time this ghastly female was leaving?

"I heard you're trying to find an old picture, sold at Gimbert's auction belonging to a Mr. Bexon?"

I gaped. You just don't ask that sort of thing in this trade. It's like asking a Great Power which other nations it really hates at a peace conference. I suddenly caught sight of Beck stepping inside Dandy Jack's. I instantly realized why Dandy hadn't kept his promise about the sketch. Beck'd heard me talking to Tinker Dill and was now arriving to buy the worthwhile stuff.

"Eh?" I responded cautiously.

"I want it," she explained. "I'm Nichole Bexon." She took hold of my arm confidingly, better and better. "I'm trying to find my uncle's things. A sketch, mainly. And two diaries. I was . . . away, you see, when his things were . . . taken to a sale. My sister cleared the house. It's so unfortunate. I heard you were trying to find them as well. A neighbor."

Good old Mary. That's the trouble. In these remote little East Anglian villages rumor does a faster job than the new electric telegraph.

"Ah, sorry, love," I said, smiling. "You'll have to try Dandy Jack." I nodded at his emporium. And, innocently thinking to get one back on poor old Dandy for changing our agreed deal in mid-scratch, I added malevolently, "He has the things you want. He won't let them go, I'm afraid. I've offered him the earth."

"Oh, *dear*." She looked almost in tears.

"Is there no way at all?" this chap asked. He'd been listening. I dragged my eyes from the lovely Nichole and noticed him.

Nichole seemed to have brought her tame male along, a real weed in Savile Row gear. The fool wore a city titfer. Honestly, some people. A hat in the Arcade's like wearing a coronet at football. You know how some couples are just not suited? Well, here was the archetypal mismatch. Her: lovely, cool, gleaming, luscious, a pure swinger. And him: neat, precise, waistcoat complete with gold watch-chain (not antique, the pathetic slob), rimless specs, glittering black shoes, and a Rolls the size of a tram. A worrier, accountant if ever I saw one. How a pill like him ever got her . . .

"No," I said.

Luckily Janie had reached (c) by now. "Mr. Lovejoy is a well-known art expert," she cut in crisply, "and even he hasn't been successful. Sorry we can't help."

She slipped into the Lagonda. It was sneering at the Rolls,

nose to nose. The Rolls wasn't really up to noticing riffraff for the moment and gazed into the distance. She gunned the engine. They got the message.

"Then what shall I do?" the beautiful Nichole said. "I must have Uncle's things back. They're nothing much. But he'd have wanted me to have them." She actually twiddled a button, one of the remaining few, on my coat.

I cleared my throat. "Er, well . . ."

"Please?" Flutter, flutter.

Women intrigue me. No, they really do. Say a woman wants ten yards of lovely Thai silk. She'd expect to have to pay for it, right? Same as a bloke wanting tobacco. Everybody knows it—you have to pay. But mention antiques and suddenly everyone wants something for nothing. Or, at the very least, a Constable or Rembrandt for a quid or two. And make no mistake, women are the worst. A man will laugh ruefully, say no hard feelings. But a woman won't. You get the whole bit, the smolder, the come-on, derision, the wheedle and finally everything they've got thrown into the fray. Born dealers, women, You have to be careful.

"Can you not help, please?" Her chap tried to smile ingratiatingly. "You've been highly recommended to us, Lovejoy, as an antique dealer. I would make it particularly worth your while. If it's a question of money . . ."

The town stilled. The universe hesitated. The High Street froze. Nobody in the known world breathed for a few lifetimes as that delightful scent of money hung in the air.

He really seemed quite pleasant after all. Charming in fact. Then Janie hauled me, literally yanking me off balance so I tumbled back into the Lagonda.

"So sorry," she called out brightly, swinging me around and slamming the door. I struggled to lower the window.

"My card," the chap said. "Phone me. Edward Rink." We were off like a Brands Hatch start. I sulked most of the way home, holding his engraved card.

It'd soon be time for Algernon's test. What a bloody day. Diddled by Dandy Jack, frogged by Beck and no nearer understanding the Bexon business, and now Algernon.

*

I'd reluctantly cleared away by the time Algernon arrived. In he came, cheerful and gormless. In his own way he's an entire miracle. A trainee dealer for six long months and still thinks Fabergé eggs are crusty chocolate.

"Good evening, Lovejoy!"

"How do." I stared morosely into his beaming face. Why was somebody who gets me so mad so bloody pleased to see me every time?

"Let us anticipate that my efforts will meet with your approval this evening!" the nerk said. He reached out and actually wrung my hand. He stripped a layer of motorcycle leathers and left them heaped in the hallway. "I am all keyed up!" he exclaimed.

"Did you read Wills?"

"Certainly, Lovejoy! And the brass instrument book. And—" he blushed—"the jokey book all over again. I appear to have been quite taken in!"

He laughed merrily as I led the way into the main room without a word. You can see why Algernon gets me down. He's always like this.

"On the table, Algernon," I cut in sourly, "are several objects."

"Right! Right!" He sprang at them, oily fingers at the ready. I caught him in mid-air and put him back.

"I shall cover all but one with a dark cloth, Algernon. You have to identify and price whichever's exposed. Okay?"

"Ah!" He raised a finger delightedly. "Your identification game!" I fetched the carriage clock across.

"You're allowed one minute. Remember?"

"Of course, Lovejoy! How absolutely right to be so precise—!"

I lifted him out of his chair by the throat, struggling for iron control.

"Algernon," I hissed. "Silence. Clam. Shut up."

"Very well! I follow exactly!" He frowned and glared intently. Then he closed his eyes to concentrate, heaven knows what with. Your modern intellectual at bay. I watched this performance wearily. I suppose it's meant to be like I do when I'm scanning, the idiot. He opened his eyes, thrilled. "Right! Ready, Lovejoy!"

"No," I said.

He concentrated hard.

"Ah! The lights!"

"Good, good, Algernon."

We lit two candles and the oil lantern before switching the electric off. I suppose there's no point in rubbing these details in too much or you'll not read on, but I have to say it. You'll all have made this mistake. What's the point in looking at Old Master paintings by neon or tungsten-filament glare? Dolphins don't do well in pasture land. Stick them in an ocean and you'll never see any living thing so full of beautiful motion. Give antiques the kind of light they're used to and you're halfway there. And for heaven's sake space the flames about the room. Never cluster natural flamelight. It's no wonder people get antiques wrong.

I sat myself down and took the time. I uncovered one small silver object. He prowled about, peering at and over it, for all the world like an amateur sleuth. I observed this weird performance with heartbreak.

"Time's up." I covered it. This is the nightmarish bit.

We sat in silence broken only by my drumming fingers, the tick of the clock and the squeaks Algernon's pores made as sweat started on his fevered brow.

"Go on, Algernon," I encouraged. "Any ideas?"

"Erm." He glanced to judge the distance to the door. "Erm. It looks . . . sort of . . . well, a *spoon*, Lovejoy."

"Precious metal? Plastic? Wood? Gilt?"

"Erm . . . silver?" he guessed desperately. "Caddy Spoon?"

"Certainly." He beamed with relief. Examine antique silver in the correct light and even Algernon can spot it. "Yes." I even smiled. "By . . . ?" He didn't know. "Three giant steps back, Algernon." His face fell a mile while I rose and uncovered all the little silvers.

He missed Hester Bateman, whizz kid of 1785. He missed the stylish Sam Massey, 1790, and the appealing work of Charles Haugham, 1781. He had omitted to learn a table of hallmarks,

55

and thought that a superb artistic piece of brilliant silverwork from Matthew Linwood's gnarled hands was plastic.

"Compare this lovely silver shellfish," I ended brokenly, "with the three in the museum tomorrow. His best work's 1808 to 1820. Look up the history of tea drinking. I'll ask you tomorrow why they never drank tea with milk or even sugar in the seventeenth century, and suchlike background gems."

"Yes, Lovejoy," he said dejectedly.

"And go around the shops that sell modern spoons. Right?" He opened his mouth. "Never mind why," I said irritably. "Just do it." I keep telling him there's no other way to learn how to spot crap, gunge and dross. I saw his blank face and wearily began to explain for the hundredth time.

*

You teach a beginner about antiques by seeing if he has any feeling for craftsmanship. It's everything. Antiques aren't alien, you see. They're extensions of mankind through time. It may seem odd that love instilled into solid materials by loving craftsmanship is the only creation of mankind to defeat time, but it's true. In holding antiques you reach across centuries and touch the very hands of genius. I don't count plastic cups or ball-point pens stamped out by a machine. Fair's fair. Man is needed.

First you look around the local furniture stores to see new furniture. Then lampshades. Then shoes. Then modern mail-order catalogues. Then mass-produced prints and paintings. Then books. Then tools. Then carpets. Then. . . . It's a terrible, frightening experience. Why do you think most modern furniture's so ghastly? And why's so much art mere dross? And fashions abysmal? And sculpture grotty? Because of Lovejoy's Law of Loving—a tin can is a tin can is a tin can, but a tin can made with loving hands glows like the Holy Grail. It deserves to be adored because the love shines through. Q.E.D., fans. Most of today's stuff could last a thousand years and never become antique simply because love's missing. They've not got it. The poor things were made without delight, human delight.

Therefore, folks, into your modern shopping precincts for a three-day penance of observation. And at every single item stop

56

and ask yourself the only question which ever mattered: "Does that look as though it was made with love, from love, to express love?" Your first day will be bad. Day Two'll be ruinous. Your third day will be the worst day of your life because you will have probably seen nothing which gets a Yes. Score zero. Nothing you see will have been made with love. It is grim—unbelievably, horrendously and frighteningly grim.

Now comes Day Four. Go, downhearted and dismal by now, into your local museum. Stand still quite a while. Then drift about and ask yourself the same question as you wander. *Now* what's the score? You already know the answer.

It's the only way to learn the antique trade. Look at rubbish, any cheap modern crud on sale now. You'll finish up hooked for life on what other people call antiques, but what I call love. Laugh if you like, but antiques are just things made full of love. The hands that produced them, in factories like flues from Hell, by some stupendous miracle of human response and feeling, managed to instill in every antique a deep hallmark of love and pride in that very act of loving.

That's why I'm an antique dealer. What I can't understand is why everybody else isn't.

*

I ended my explanation. Algernon was goggling. He's heard it umpteen times.

Algernon failed that whole evening miserably. He failed on the precious early Antoine Gaudin photograph I'd borrowed. He failed on a rare and valuable *Peacock's New Double Dissection and History of England and Wales*, 1850, by Gall and Inglis of Paternoster Square ("What a tatty old jigsaw, Lovejoy!"), and a child's George IV complete tea set, almost microscopically small—the teapot's a quarter of an inch long—brilliantly carved from hardwood and very, very costly. Of this last Algernon soared to his giddiest height yet, asking brightly, "What kind of plastic is it, Lovejoy?"

I slung him out after that, unable to go on. I'd not laid a finger on him. Will power.

The world would have to wait with bated breath for Algernon's judgment of paired water ewers, Wedgwood and Bentley polished black basalt, which I'd borrowed to include in his test. But I was especially keen not to hear him on the film transparency of a tortuously elaborate weapon by that genius Minamoto Tauguhiro. I couldn't bear hearing him say it was a fancy dagger for slicing bread.

He donned his motorbike leathers. I pushed him forcibly into the dark garden.

"I expect you're letting me off early because I was doing so well," he said merrily. He believes every word.

"Sure, sure."

"Will you please inform Uncle how successful I was with those sugar ladles?" he asked at the door. "He will be so hugely delighted." His uncle pays me for teaching the goon.

I wonder where all my patience comes from, honestly. "I'll tell him you're making your usual progress, Algernon."

"*Thank you,* Lovejoy!" he exclaimed joyously. "You know, eventually I anticipate to be almost as swift as your good self—"

I shut the door. There's a limit.

        *

Normally I'd stroll up to the pub to wash all that Algernon-induced trauma out of my mind. This particular night I was too late to escape. There was a knock at my door.

"Nichole. What—?"

"Kate," she said. Her smile made it the coldest night of the year. "The wicked sister."

"Oh, come in." She was slightly taller than Nichole but the same coloring.

"No, thank you. You're Lovejoy?" I nodded. You feel so daft just standing holding a door open, don't you. You can't shut it and you can't go out or back in. "I want to ask you not to help my sister," she said carefully. "She . . . her judgment is sometimes, well, not too reliable, you understand."

"I haven't helped her," I explained. "She wanted a sketch and some—"

"Some rubbish," Kate cut in. "Uncle was a kindly man, but

given to making up fanciful tales. I don't want my sister influenced."

"About his other belongings," I began hopefully.

"Very ordinary furniture, very cheap, very modern," she stated, cold as ever. "And now all sold. You do understand about Nichole?"

"Sure," I said. She said goodnight and drove into the darkness in an elderly Mini. I sighed and locked up. I seemed to be alienating the universe.

*

I've told you all this the way I have because it was the last quiet time there was in the whole business. I realized during the rest of that evening that something was rapidly going wrong in my humdrum normal life. Looking back, I don't see to this day what else I could have done.

The murder honestly wasn't my fault, and I don't think the other deaths were, either. Honest.

7

Janie bounced in early next morning. Her husband had been called away to the city for the day, the early train. It wasn't any good, though. The feeling was still on me. I sent her packing. She was wild and refused to go but I picked her up and chucked her outside on the porch. She even tried scratching my eyes as I slammed the door. To be fair, I hinted I'd work to do, quite politely. She even rushed around to the back. I reached the bolt first, pulled the curtains and with Janie banging on the door hauled up my paving. She'd be mad for days. She'd brought a picnic basket, as if there'd be time for that sort of thing.

Down in the priest's hole the cardboard box's contents seemed even more pathetic. I unfolded the small ledged Regency table, a godsend in these days of wobbling warping junk, and poured the buttons out. I started on them with a lens and prism. It takes time. The photos were 1930s, old churches, a beach, a boardinghouse. An hour later I reached the first medal, the old "ration gong" of the War. Ordinary. There seemed not a single hint among the lot.

I have twenty shoe boxes full of what history got up to, but I couldn't find a trace of any Lady Isabella. The books showed nothing special under the microscope, no microdots, no secret inks, no oiled-in watermarks. I cleared up and got ready to leave. The box was better left in the hidden cellar. When I came out into the garden I found Janie had driven off in a huff. Now I'd have to walk up into the village and wait for our single market bus about noon. Why have women no patience? I had no more cheese for the robin. I borrowed some budgie seed and told them I owed it.

"The message is in the words." I told the robin. "And they're only a list of places, right? All you need to do is visit each place and you'd find where he's put the Roman stuff. It should be obvious. Easy."

Easy. Even if they were in the Isle of Man, and me with only the busfare to town. I'd walk back. Still, things were definitely looking up for Lovejoy Antiques, Inc. At least I'd a ray of hope now.

"I'll go and do a bit to the painting," I told the robin.

Inevitably the phone rang.

"Lovejoy. I hope you don't mind?" Nichole.

"No. Glad to hear you."

We held the pause. There's a sudden affinity between two people sometimes when nothing really needs saying.

"I . . . I was ringing to ask your help. The sketch and the rubbish from Uncle James."

"Dandy Jack has them," I told her carefully. "I did some work for him but he wouldn't part with the sketch."

"I see," she said icily. "Are you sure your girlfriend hasn't bought them for you?"

"No, look, love," I was saying when she slammed the phone down.

I went out to work on my painting, whistling. She'd come round.

In the back garden near where Manton and Wilkinson fly I have this workshop. The big work of the moment was transferring a genuine 1774 Wilson painting to a new canvas. I goggled up, apron, mask and all. Janie laughs at my garb, but what's wrong with being not stupid?

When your superb antique painting's rotting to hell you must act. If you're a beginner, take it to an expert for advice. This painting's Richard Wilson, possibly the most underrated grand master. I'd found it being used to pad the back seat of an old

Austin Ruby. The bloke thought I was off my head. He was the sort who would chuck away a First Folio and keep the string.

If a painting's canvas is literally falling to bits you've a choice, of simply (figure of speech, that—it's really very complicated) rebacking with a new canvas, or of lifting the old delicate work of art *off* the canvas and putting it on a new one. This isn't fraud. It saves a precious thing for another three centuries and is therefore essential. My method is to stretch small-grain gauze until it's even, then stick it carefully to the painting's face. (My glue's secret. Find your own.) Several layers of paper tissue stuck to the gauze, and you now remove the painting, still on its decrepit canvas, from the wood stretcher. After days of drying, tissue-gauze surface downward; then, on an absolutely even bench, in the right wooden frame to hold it still, you gently caress the old canvas away. It takes maybe three months to a year's spare-time caressing. It's not much. For a beautiful, luscious—or even an ugly—antique oil painting it's worth every second. You need to remove the debris as you go. Some use pumice stone, others special flat-face drills. I use me and a special powder I make up myself. Then stick a new canvas on any way you like. Tip: if you ever do it, be careful to announce the painting's been re-canvassed or you'll not get a bean for it. You can't blame the honest old public for being worried if they see yesterday's date stamped on the canvas of a genuine Constable. They're a very shrewd and suspicious mob.

I was caressing away when somebody coughed at my elbow.

"There's a bell at the gate," I said angrily, not looking up.

"So sorry." Great. Nichole's bloke, your actual Edward Rink.

Eventually I rose, stepped carefully back from the bench and turned. He was there, hesitant but determined. He must have left his car in the lane.

"I called in Dandy Jack's early this morning."

"Survive, did he?"

"He says he sold the sketch."

"That's life," I said, wondering if Dandy actually had.

He pulled out a gold case and did the fire ritual. No kind offer of a fag to one of the world's workers.

"To a young lady." His bottled eyes quivered indignantly. "I think it was your young lady, Lovejoy." Two little disks of red glowed on his cheeks.

"Oh?" Typical of Dandy. I bet he'd really sold it to Beck. Dealers are rarely truthful about these innocent details. I decided not to say this, and to mention nothing about Nichole's phone call.

"And the diaries Nichole's uncle wrote. I understand from Dandy Jack you have them."

"You do?" I was thinking, what the hell's going on?

"Now, Lovejoy." He was trying so hard. I watched curiously. "I'm willing to pay for them. You—you have no car, I believe."

"True."

"Nichole treasures her uncle's things." He swallowed shakily. There were beads of sweat on his forehead. "I'm willing to buy you a popular car. In exchange."

"What's so precious about them, Rink?"

"Nichole's sister. She . . ." his voice hardened. "They don't see quite eye to eye. Kate's often . . . unpleasant to Nichole. It happens in some families. I heard she called on you last night, Lovejoy."

I eyed him. How did he know that?

"Yes. And practically told me to get stuffed. Anyway, it's a lot of money for two old scrapbooks, isn't it?"

"Lovejoy," he said, whitening round his lips. "You *will* let me have them. And obtain your girl friend's cooperation. Or else."

"Eh?" I couldn't believe my ears.

"You heard, Lovejoy." The pillock mistook my amazement for awe.

"Are you trying to—?"

"Threaten?" His little eyes flicked around the garden, the shed. "Yes."

"You? *Me?*" I asked fascinated. I'd seen some rum customers in my time, but this . . .

"You." He flung his cigarette down and stood on it—note, not stamped or ground it in with his heel. Simply stood. I should have been thinking at the time. I'd have seen what sort of a swine he was. "You have a choice, Lovejoy. Money plus physical well-being. Or poverty and . . ."

"And?" I prompted hilariously.

"And pain, Lovejoy," he said gravely.

"Look," I tried to say, but this wart actually tapped my chest to shut me up.

"You look, Lovejoy." Worse, his breath was unfortunate. "I'm a businessman. I can play rough. I have the money to get things done. By others. Tougher than you. And you are strapped, practically in the soup queue."

Well, I laughed. Honestly, I was helpless. Here was this nerk threatening a bloke like me. I've been in more dust-ups than dances, so maybe you can't blame me for the hilarity. I had to sit down on the orange-box. He stood there, ashen.

"Listen, mate," I managed to gasp at last. "Dandy Jack's having you on. If it was a bird bought it, she wasn't mine. And," I finished, sobering, "if you'd asked more politely I'd have sold you the diaries for a couple of quid. As it is, get lost."

"So Dandy Jack was lying?"

"How the hell should I know?"

He looked me over, a really cold fish.

"The next time we meet you'll beg me to accept them as a gift, Lovejoy," he said portentously. "You've been adequately warned."

"Sure, sure."

He turned and stalked off.

I was still laughing when I caught the noon bus.

*

On the way to town I found myself thinking about an old chap possibly finding a coffin full of antiques.

You may believe that expecting to find (as opposed to buying) is something of a pipe dream. Long may you so believe, because that lessens the chances of you doing any finding. The odds for me then get better. From the bottom of my atherosclerotic heart take my tip: keep looking. And above all keep expecting. When all's said and done, those London bankers who found that stash of Lord Byron's poems in their cellars weren't out for a casual stroll, were they? They were tidying up old deed boxes. Hence the now legendary discovery of documents and poems from 1820, the Scrope Davies find (of "inaccurate memory," as Byron called this celebrated Dandy—note the capital letter; they were very particular). So when I hear of "lucky" finds I always think to myself, what were they doing looking in the first place? And I mean them all. The nine-year-old Yorkshire lad who found that priceless Saxon longsword in the silt of the stream at Gilling West. The two Colchester children who dug down to the Romano-British temple in Lexden. The East Anglian farmer who noticed a large circle of wheat standing tall and perfect during a recent wilting drought and had the sense to measure the circle carefully with his hobnails for thinking about after the harvest was gathered in—and discovered the burial tomb circle of one of King Tasciovanus' tributary kings. And me: I once bought an "old" Victorian knitting needle found locally from Wilkie's shop (he's navigation and naval instruments of the eighteenth century) and "an iron Georgian drinking cup" from Harry's in our High Street on the selfsame day—because I can smell a Roman legion doctor's instruments at a thousand leagues. So look with courageous expectation, folks. You may have a king buried in your own back yard.

I wistfully remembered the story of the lovely, mystic Beaworth Box, holding a good ten thousand dazzling coins from A.D. 1087. It was a small lead box, very like a coffin. Like the Cuerdale Chest, complete with its precious silver ornaments. Like the Flaxton Box. I can't go on. It's too painful. And really delicious hoards have been found on the Isle of Man, like the two at Andreas.

See how you can talk yourself around?

"This is as far as we go, mate," the conductor was saying, giving me a nudge.

"Then I'll get off," I said, and I did.

*

In town I phoned Janie. Luckily she herself answered. I asked her if she'd gone to Dandy's and bought the Burne-Jones sketch. She said no, still mad at me. That made Nichole, Janie, Nichole's private nutter Edward Rink, Mary the housewife, Kate, and eighteen debtors all blazing at me, just within two days. I honestly do try but sometimes nobody else bothers. There are times like that.

8

Early afternoon. I was in Margaret's shop in the Arcade. She and I had been good friends when Janie'd happened, which was a bit tough. There were a score of customers drifting along the covered pavement, a few in and out of Margaret's. I jokingly accuse her of showing herself off to get customers in. Like all women she has attraction, but I like Margaret especially. No bitterness and a lot of compassion. She could teach a million things to a lot of younger women.

Margaret had picked up a job lot of eighteenth-century household stuff I'd promised to price. We sat in her glass-fronted area as I sorted through. It was interesting enough but low grade. Best was a collection of Regency pipe stubbers in the form of gloved hands, erotic figurines, tiny pipe racks, people, tennis rackets, rings, shapely legs, wine bottles. You get them in silver, brass, ivory, pewter, even hardwood and glass. She'd got twenty, by some miracle. Incidentally, always go for collections rather than items. I also liked a box of braided matches, R. Bell & Co., the elegant braid still on every single match—quaint Victorian elegance if you like, but fascinating.

"Not bad, Margaret."

"I was lucky." She eyed me. "Anything you like?"

"Everything." I couldn't keep the bitterness out.

Her hand touched my arm.

"It's a spell of bad luck, that's all, Lovejoy." She paused. "Anything I can do?"

I pulled a scarey face to show I couldn't care less. Women who offer help need watching. Just then Patrick hurtled in with a fit of vapors and flung himself down on a William IV diamond seat, a nice pale oak with very few markings.

"Lovejoy!" he screamed, holding out his handbag to me.

"Yes?" I gazed apprehensively at his gilt plastic accessory.

"Well?" he screeched. "Get my smelling salts out, you great fool!"

"No. You." I never go along with his hysterics. Tantrums are personal things.

"Whatever's the matter, Patrick?" Margaret did it and set about restoring him.

"Not too close with the little bottle, dear," he snapped. "I need reviving, not gassing."

"What is it?"

"Dandy Jack." Patrick swooned backward. "He's been run over. Outside. I just can't *tell* you." But he did, emphasizing his own reactions most of all. In seemed Dandy was sprinting to the Red Lion as usual when he was knocked down by a car. It didn't stop.

"Am I pale as absolute death?" Patrick asked fearfully of all and sundry. He peeped into his handbag mirror.

"You *are* pale, dear," from Margaret. He leaned back and closed his eyes.

"I'm positively *drained* to my anklestraps."

"Did somebody take the number?"

"Hardly, dear." Patrick patted his cheeks. "We were fainting like flitted flies."

"Bloody idiot," I said. He glared.

"Shut your face, you great oaf, Lovejoy," he spat. "If you'd been through what I've just undergone—"

"You only watched," I pointed out. "Dandy got done."

"How do you *bear* him?" Patrick cooed to Margaret. "Uncouth ape."

Lily came trotting after, as always, the embodiment of sacrificial desire. Hope beats eternal in the human breast but I honestly wonder what the hell for, sometimes. She was more precise than Patrick had been.

"They've taken Dandy to hospital," she said breathlessly. "He looked really awful, blood everywhere."

"Don't!" Patrick moaned, doing his swoon.

"Are you all right, lovie?" Lily rallied around him.

"Sod him," I said. "The point is will Dandy be all right?"

"Charming!" Patrick instantly recovered enough to glare daggers at me.

"I don't know, Lovejoy." Lily dabbed anxiously with a tissue at Patrick, who jerked away.

"Mind my mascara!" he screeched. "Silly cow!"

"Sorry, dear," Lily was saying when I pecked Margaret's cheek and moved off.

"If Patrick wants to do the entire scene," I said, "lend him an asp."

"May your ceramics turn to sand, Lovejoy!" he called spitefully after me.

"Shush, lovie! Try to rest!" from Lily.

"Why does everybody *hate* me so?" he was wailing as I left the Arcade. I suppose it takes all sorts.

The hospital is a few streets away. You cut alongside the ancient steps through the remains of the Roman wall. As I hurried among the crowds I couldn't help thinking that too many things were happening too quickly all of a sudden. In spite of my hurry I couldn't help pausing at Dig Mason's, the poshest of the Arcade's antique windows. Pride of place was given to a delightful veneered drop-sided portmanteau. It contained an entire set of dining cutlery, china service, glass tableware down to cruets and serviette rings. Everything was slightly smaller-sized than normal. My heart melted. Perfect. Dig beamed out at me through the window miming an invitation to make an offer. I gave him the thumbs down and hurried away. He'd labelled it "Lady's travelling dining case. Complete. Victorian." All wrong. I'd have labelled it "Officer's mess dining portmanteau. Complete. 1914–15. World War I," and been correct. The poor sods were made to provide complete mess gear and often their own china and cutlery in the Royal Flying Corps. As I hurried along I prayed Dig

68

wouldn't realize his mistake before I got some money from somewhere. He'd underpriced it a whole hundred per cent.

I looked among the cars but there was no sign of Janie. She must have decided to stay away in a temper. Typical. Just as you need women they get aggro. They make me mad. They lack organization.

*

Helen was at the hospital. She came over as soon as I entered the foyer. Funny what impressions hospitals leave. All I can remember is a lot of prams, some children and an afternoon footballer being wheeled along with his leg in plaster.

"He's not too good, Lovejoy," Helen said.

"I'm glad you came."

She shot a look at me and together we climbed to the second floor. I never know who's boss nurse anymore. Once it was easy—dark blue were sisters, pale blue stripes nurses and doctors in white. Now they seem as lost as the rest of us. Helen accosted a matron who turned out to be a washer-up. We made three mistakes before we stood at the foot of Dandy Jack's bed.

He appeared drained, newly and spectacularly clean and utterly defenceless. Drips dripped. Tubes tubed into and out of more orifices than God ever made. Bottles collected or dispensed automatically. It seemed nothing more than one colossal act, a tableau without purpose or message. Dandy Jack was never a divvie, but even boozy dealers deserve to live.

"Did you see the accident?" a tired young house doctor asked. I said no.

"I did. From a distance." Helen linked her arm with mine. I think we both felt under scrutiny, somehow allowed in under sufferance.

"Did he go unconscious instantly?"

"Yes. The car pushed him along quite several yards," Helen told him. "It wasn't going all that fast."

"Did Dandy see it?" I asked her. She shook her head.

The doctor moved us out of the ward with a head wag.

"Are you next of kin?"

We stared, hesitated before answering.

"Well, he has none, doctor," Helen said at last. "As far as we know."

"He's—seriously injured, you see." He asked us to leave a phone number.

We finished up giving Margaret's. Helen meant, but didn't say, that she'd know to reach me through Janie somehow. On the way back to the High Street we carefully disengaged arms just in case. Helen told me the car was a big old Rover.

"I could have sworn, Lovejoy ..." Helen paused. "I had an idea the driver might have been ... that chap you were talking to outside Dandy's."

"The one with the blonde?" Rink.

"Yes, but a different car."

"Well," I said carefully, "one doesn't use one's very best for dealing with the vulgar mob, does one?"

"I could be wrong, I suppose."

"You could." I left it at that.

"I'll tell Margaret we gave her home number," Helen said. She paused as we made to part. "Lovejoy."

"What?"

"Ring me." She met my eyes. "Whenever."

"If I come into money," I quipped.

"Have you eaten?" she examined my face. "You're gaunt."

"It's the ascetic life I lead." We looked at each other another moment. "See you, Helen."

"Yes."

*

I was wondering, can a duck egg like Rink be so savage? Then I thought, aren't we all?

An hour later I discovered my phone had been cut off, which only goes to show the phone people are as savage as the rest of us.

9

That afternoon I'd never been so famished. Hunger's all right but bad for morale. I combed the cottage for provisions and ended up with a quarter-full tin of powdered milk, a tiny piece of cheese I'd overlooked, one small cooking apple, some limp celery, a bottle of sauce and five grotty teabags. Hardly nosh on the Elizabethan scale. Just as well Henry wasn't due today. He'd have started on the divan. I glanced at my nonedible walnut carriage clock and decided to call on Squaddie. He's always good for a calorie.

First, however, I would cerebrate for a minute or two. This Bexon business was starting to niggle. I strolled into the garden. On the face of it, you couldn't call it much of a problem. I sat on the garden steps near the budgies' flight, whistling to think better.

An old geezer dies, leaving behind a scrawled tale telling how he'd had a holiday and found some ruins or other. A mosaic. And a gold or two, Lovejoy. Don't forget them. Then he leaves his story in duplicate. Well, big deal. Two nieces explained that. Clearly one booklet each and a funny drawing of Lady Isabella chucked in for luck. From the way Nichole's henchman Rink had behaved none of us knew any more than that. I chuckled at the memory of his absurd threat, making Manton and Wilkinson look around irritably at my whistling's sudden halt. Then I thought of Dandy Jack.

"Sorry, lads," I told them. "Just thinking."

We all resumed, me sitting on the cold stones and the birds trilling on their enclosed branches. Singing makes their chests bulge so they rock about. Ever noticed that? It's a miracle they don't fall off. I expect their feet keep tighter hold on the twigs than you'd think from a casual look.

The problem lay of course in what we were all busy guessing. Nichole's wealthy hero obviously guessed an enormous crock of gold somewhere. Greedy sod. He was already at least a two-Rolls man. Janie guessed I was wasting my time again when I should have been seducing her away from her posh hubby. Dandy Jack was guessing that his Burne-Jones drawing would settle his boozing bills for some time to come, and he was right. Always assuming he got better and those bouncy nurses let him loose.

"Manton." He looked at me in silence. "What," I asked, "am I guessing? That's the real problem, isn't it?"

They glanced at each other, then back at me. We all thought hard.

"You're right," I said, got out my rusty old bike and hit the road. I had to pump its front tire up first.

*

About three miles from my cottage tidal creeks begin. Low-lying estuaries, woods, sloping green fields, orchards and beautiful undulating countryside blending with the mighty blue ocean and getting on my wick, though not everybody sees sense like I do. Even though it was quite early a couple of anglers were ruminating on the Infinite along the Goldhammer inlet, and some nut was trying to get the total boredom of the scene on canvas— tomorrow's antique. Or even today's? I pedalled past with a friendly greeting. The artist was pleased and shouted a goodday, but the anglers were mad because a bicycle bell warns the fish away. I gave it a couple of extra rings.

Cheered by my day's good turn, I rode out onto the strood. That's a road sticking out from the shore across a short reach of sea to an island. You can easily pass over when the sea's out but you have to wade chest-deep when the tide's in. People who live on these low windswept islands have the times of the tides written out and stuck inside their car doors. Always assuming you have a car, I thought nastily. There's a lifebelt hung on the wooden railing so you get the message. The North Sea's no pond.

This particular strood's about half a mile long. Three or four boats lay sprawled close to the roadway on the exposed mud-flats among reed wisps. A couple of fishing ketches were standing out to sea in the cold light. But the boat I was heading for would never sail again. It came into view half way across, a blue lifeboat converted for houseboat living and sensibly rammed as far up as possible on the highest inlet out of the sea marshes.

Squaddie was in and cooking. I could tell from the gray smoke pouring from the iron stack. I whistled through my fingers. He likes a good warning.

"After some grub, Lovejoy?" his voice quavered from the weatherbeaten cabin. He's getting on.

"Yes. Get it ready," I yelled back and slung my bicycle among the hawthorns.

He has a double plank with railings sloping from the old tow-path to his deck. How lucky I'd called at mealtime. Frying bacon and eggs. He gives me that and some of those malt flakes and powdered milk, my usual once a week.

"Hiyer, Squaddie."

"Hello, Lovejoy."

An old boy can get about a lot even if he's blind. Squaddie used to be our best antique dealer (me excepted) till his eyes gave in. A curious chap, wise enough for more than me to use as an oracle.

"You're a day early."

"Not brewed up yet, Squaddie? I'm gasping."

Squaddie scratched his stubble and listened acutely to the momentary silence between us. His sightless rheumy eyes could still move. It was a bit disconcerting in the small cabin, to catch a sudden flash of white sclera from a face sightless five years and more. I slued across the tilted floor and sat where I could see to seaward.

"You on to something, Lovejoy?"

I shrugged evasively, remembered in time he couldn't see shrugs and said I wasn't sure.

"Good or bad?"

"Neither."

He cackled at that and mixed powdered milk.

"It's got to be one or the other," he corrected, shuffling dexterously from galley to table and laying for me as well. "Antiques are either lovely and real or imitation and useless."

"It can be neither," I said. "It can be funny."

"Oh. Like that, eh?"

While we started to nosh I told him about Bexon, the forgery, the lovely Nichole and her pal, Dandy Jack's accident and the diaries. You can't blame me for missing out Janie and the leading details of old Bexon's holiday trip because Squaddie still does the occasional deal. Nothing wrong with being careful.

"How does it sound?" I asked him.

"Rum. Where's the picture?"

"Dandy Jack kept it—after I'd sorted for him."

He laughed, exposing a row of rotten old teeth.

"Typical. That Dandy."

"Did you ever hear of Bexon?"

"Aye. Knew him." He stirred his egg cleverly into a puddle with a bread stick. You couldn't help staring. How does a blind man know exactly where the yolk is? "Tried to get him to copy a Wright canvas for me. Seascape. He wouldn't."

"Money?"

"Not on your life." Squaddie did his odd eye-rolling trick again. Maybe it eases them. "Bexon was honest."

"Was he off his rocker?"

"Him? A northern panel bowler?"

That said all. Panel bowlers are nerveless team players on crown bowling greens. They never gamble themselves, but they carry immense sums wagered on them by spectators at every match. You can't do that and be demented.

"When did you see him last, Squaddie?" I could have kicked myself even if it is only a figure of speech. Squaddie didn't seem to notice.

"I forget." He scraped the waste together and handed it to me to chuck out of the cabin window. "He was just off somewhere on holiday. Isle of Man, I think."

"What was he?"

"Trade? Engineer, craftsman and all that. Local firm."

"Go on digs?" We suffer a lot from epidemics of amateur archeologists hereabouts. And professional ones who are much, much worse.

"He wasn't one for hunting Camelot at weekends, if that's what you mean, Lovejoy." He was laughing as he poured, thick and tarry. Lovely. "Nieces wouldn't let him. Real firebrands, they are."

I caught myself thinking, Maybe that explains why Bexon found his hoard on the Isle of Man and not locally. Almost as if I was actually coming to believe his little diaries were a perfectly true record. You have to watch yourself in this game. Persuasion's all very well for others.

We chatted then about antiques in general. He asked after friends, Jimmo, the elegant Patrick, Jenny and Harry Bateman, Big Frank. We talked of prices and who were today's rascals (plenty) and who weren't (very few).

"How's Algernon?" he finally asked me, chuckling evilly. Well he might.

"Bloody horrible."

"He'll improve, Lovejoy."

I forgot to tell you Algernon is Squaddie's nephew.

"He won't. Green as the proverbial with the brains of a rocking horse."

"He's your bread and butter for the moment, Lovejoy." It was Squaddie who'd foisted him on me as soon as I went bust, to make him the world's greatest antique dealer for a few quid a month. Your actual Cro-Magnon. I'd never have taken a trainee in a million years if Squaddie hadn't taken the liberty. It's called friendship. I visit Squaddie weekly to report our complete lack of progress.

"What's he on?"

"Glass. Musical instruments. He doesn't know the difference."

"You cruel devil, Lovejoy. He'll learn." That's what blood does for you. You can't spot your own duds.

"He's a right lemon. Should be out earning his keep like a growing lad, van-driving."

"One day he'll surprise you."

"Only surprise?" I growled. "He frightens the frigging daylights out of me."

"Not need the money anymore, Lovejoy?" Squaddie cackled slyly. I swallowed.

"I'll keep on with him," I conceded at last. He passed my notes over. I earn every farthing.

"He's got the gift," Squaddie said determinedly. "He'll be a divvie like you."

I sighed heavily and thanked him for the nosh. Before I left I arranged to skip tomorrow's visit. "Unless," I added cruelly as a parting salvo, "Algernon's skills mushroom overnight."

"They will," he promised. "Anyway, good luck with the Roman stuff, Lovejoy."

"Cheers, Squaddie." I paused on the gangplank, thinking hard. "Did you say Roman?" I called back. No answer. I called louder, "Who said anything about Roman stuff?"

"Didn't you?" he quavered from the cabin. He'd already started washing up.

"Not a word."

"You mentioned digging, archeology, Lovejoy. That's Roman."

"So it is," I said. Well, it is, isn't it?

But I'd said nothing to young Algernon at the cottage. Nothing could have got back to Squaddie through him. Maybe it was an inspired guess. There are such things, aren't there? We said our farewells all over again, ever so polite.

I got my bicycle. My picture of Bexon was building up: a highly skilled painter, known among a select few old friends in the antique trade. A good quiet family man. Cool under stress. And honest with it, to boot. Still, I thought, pedalling down the marshes to the strood again in the cutting east wind, nobody's perfect. I started ringing my bicycle bell to warn the fish that those two anglers were still bent on murder. The artist waved, grinning. The anglers didn't. Perhaps they thought me unsporting.

I pedalled off the strood onto the mainland. The only difference between cycling and being in Janie's Lagonda is that she's not there to keep saying take your hand off my knee.

    *

Now I had money. Not much, but any at all is more than twice nothing. The trouble is people have to *see* money, or they start jumping to all sorts of conclusions. This trade's very funny. Reputations matter.

The White Hart was fairly full, everbody talking all at once as usual. I paused for a second, rapturously inhaling the booze-laden smoke and gazing around. Jenny and Harry were huddled close, uptight. I'd heard Jenny was seeing some wealthy bloke on the sly. Maybe Harry had tumbled, or maybe they'd bounced a deal wrong. Well, antiques occasionally caused difficulties, I snickered to myself. Tinker Dill was there, holding forth against the bar to a cluster of other grubby barkers. I still wonder who'd bought that round. Helen was resting, long of leg and full of curves, on a stool like women with good legs do and gave me a half-smile and a nod. She's always exhaling smoke. She even smokes in bed. (Er, I mean, I *suppose* she probably does.) Margaret was in, too. I waved. Big Frank wasn't in yet. Patrick was showing off to anyone who cared. Lily gave me a wave. She'd been to a silver sale in Lavenham that day.

"What'll you have, Lily?"

Only Ted the barman didn't eye the money in my hand. He assimilates feelings about solvency by osmosis.

"No. My turn."

"I insist." I had a pint, Lily a mysterious rum thing. I asked if she'd visited Dandy in hospital.

"I went," she said. "Patrick would have, but he's not very—strong."

"That plump nurse'll hose Dandy down a bit, eh?" I chuckled.

"Lovejoy," Lily said carefully. "I don't know if Dandy's going to be, well, all right."

"Not get better? Dandy Jack?" I smiled at that. "He's tough as old boots. He'll make it. Did the Old Bill catch the maniac?"

"Not yet." Her voice lowered. "They're saying in the Arcade it looked like—" , .

"If it was Rink he'll have a hundred alibis."

The interlude done with, Lily turned to her own greatest problem, who was now lecturing Ted on lipstick. ("That *orange* range is such a poxy risk, Teddie dear!")

"What am I going to do, Lovejoy?"

"Give him the sailor's elbow," I advised.

She gazed at Patrick's blue rinse with endearment. Patrick glanced over, saw us and coo-eed extravagantly.

"Do you like it, Lovejoy?" he shrieked, waggling his fingers.

"Er . . . ?"

"The new nail varnish, dear! Mauve!" He emitted an outraged yelp and turned away. "Oh, isn't he positively moronic?"

"Would you speak to him, Lovejoy?" Lily begged. She'd made sure nobody was in earshot. "He treats me like dirt."

"Chuck him, love."

"He admires you. He'd listen. He says you're the only proper dealer we've got."

"That's a laugh."

"It's true," she said earnestly. "He's even been trying to help you. He's been making enquiries about Bexon all afternoon."

"Eh?"

"For you, Lovejoy." Lily smiled fondly in Patrick's direction. "Even though there's nothing in it for him. He went down to Gimbert's." The auction rooms where Bexon's belongings went. "One day he'll realize I love him—"

"Does your husband know?" I asked, thinking, since when does an antique dealer do anything for nothing. Even one like Patrick. He used to deal in goldsmithy (antique gold) till that gold price business ten years ago.

"Not yet," she admitted. "When I'm sure of Patrick I'll explain. He'll understand."

"It's more than I do," I said. "Look, love. Can't you see that Patrick's—er—?"

"It's a phase," she countered. "Only a phase."

Jill Jenkins made her entrance, a nimble fortyish. She's medieval, early mechanicals, toys, manuscripts and dress items. I like her because she's good, really as expert as any dealer we have locally. Not a divvie, just an expert. I'd never seen her boyfriend before, but then I'd never seen any of Jill's boyfriends before. They all look the same to me. Only the names change, about once every twelve hours. Tinker Dill once told me he can tell the new ones by their ear lobes. Jill picks them up on the harbor wharf. Our port can just about keep pace with Jill's appetite, as long as one of our estuary fogs doesn't hold the ships up. Her husband has the farm in Stirling, very big on agriculture.

Well, whatever turns you on, but there are some rum marital arrangements about these days.

"Lovejoy! My poppet!" I got a yard of rubberoid lips and a waft of expensive perfume. "And Lily too! How nice!" she added absently, glancing around with the occasional yoo-hoo and finger flutter.

"Hiyer, Jill."

"This is—" she started an introduction—"what is it, darling?"

"Richard," the lad said. "Rum and black currant."

"Richard," Jill said, pleased somebody had remembered. "That's it. He's left his boat down in the water."

"How very wise," Lily said sweetly, moving away. "Now he'll know where to find it, won't he?"

"Ship," Richard said sourly. "Not boat. Ship."

"I hear," Jill said, taking my arm and coming too close, "Lovejoy's roamin' after Roman." She had on a beautiful Egyptian scarab brooch, genuine. My bell clamored.

"Roman stuff?" I said calmly. "Whoever told you that?"

"Big Frank," she admitted, not batting any one of her false eyelashes. "And that whore Jenny Bateman." She caught Jenny's eye the same instant and trilled a greeting through the saloon. The Batemans waved.

Ted fetched Richard's drink. Jill always has ginger wine. They allow Jill's drink on the slate. For some reason they don't trust the rest of us.

"Lily just said that," I said. "Funny how things get about."

"Any special Roman stuff, dear?"

"Must have been a misunderstanding, Jill," I replied. I was distinctly uncomfortable.

"Did Popplewell help you clear it up?" she asked roguishly.

"I was only doing a routine call at the Castle," I said.

"If you've the money," she said, suddenly businesslike, "I've some Roman bronze statuary. No gold coins, though. What time're you due back, William?"

"Couple of hours. And it's Richard."

"That'll give us just long enough. Then I'll run you back to your boat."

"Ship," I said for him, got another moist plonk from Jill's mouth and escaped.

10

On the way back I called in Ruffler's bakery, four meat-and-potato pasties and two flour cakes. It's very interesting being poor at this level. You'd think that you'd start buying foods again in exactly the reverse order you gave them up. It's not true. For example, I'd not tasted butter or margarine for four months at the cottage. And here I was with a few quid, splashing out on a quarter of marge and a pot of honey. Big spender. For sheer erg value I bought a dozen eggs, a tin of powdered milk and a slab of Lancashire cheese the size of a Queen Anne *escritoire*. Manton and Wilkinson had seed forever so I got two loaves, a cob and a farmhouse. That made a hell of a hole in Squaddie's few quid. I dithered about a tin of corned beef and a custard but decided not to go mad. My belly would be shocked enough as it was. I bought tinned sausages and salad cream for Henry.

I felt so proud having a proper tea. You do, don't you. Even got my tablecloth out and laid it. It's Victorian embroidered white linen, lovely. White-on-white's stylish needlework, but hell to iron. (Tip: Use an old nonelectric flatiron. Don't think that electric's always right just because it's easy.) I washed the cutlery and found a napkin from somewhere. My Indian bone-and-rosewood inlaid tea tray made everything look really sophisticated. If anyone had come in they'd have thought how homely it all was. Funny how a person's mind works. I put the margarine and honey in a prominent position so they could be seen clearly by unexpected visitors. They'd think it was routine. To reinforce the image I put both loaves and flour cakes on show. The message for the casual observer: that Lovejoy lives really well, always a choice of bread. I had two pasties, hotted up. The others went away for the morrow.

As I stoked up even my old table manners returned. No elbows on the table, knife and fork demurely parallel. I was charming, and not a little narked nobody came to witness the exhibition.

That done, I went to see Manton and Wilkinson. Darkness was about to fall on the valley. From the cottage you can see the lights along the Lexton village road some four miles away. There's a cluster of cottages, the river and the railway about a mile closer. At dusk it's quite pretty, but coolish and always misty. A faint foggish air drifts in from the estuary, slow and rather ominous sometimes. That makes the lights gleam prettily for a few minutes. Then you notice the cold dankness hanging to cut off the last of the valley's dusk, and the day has ended. The night is a swamp through which sounds fail to carry. Trees loom wider and hedges crowd close.

I told Manton and Wilkinson goodnight. They were locked in well. Odd, but I distinctly remember wishing for once that I'd a dog. One of the villagers has two geese. He says they're better than any watchdog.

Algernon was due soon for his test. I'd have to get ready. I went in and shut the cottage door.

Outside the lights of all the world must have seemed to dowse with a slam.

*

It was late. I'd given Algernon his quiz. Results: dreadful. I'd been teaching him the difference between jet, black jadeite and black pigmented acrylate resins. (Today's hint: go for nineteenth-century Whitby jet brooches if you're wanting the very best. They're worth the premium. And genuine jet's practically impossible to copy.) He'd suggested the easiest way's burning—jet burns, you see. I'd explained that keeping the jewelry intact's

81

preferable to a heap of ash. I'd shown him how I measure specific gravity (jet's not more than 1.40, which is peanuts to jadeite's 3.30 or even more; acrylate resin's never far from 1.18.). It's not foolproof, but you're a lot nearer the truth knowing details like this. I sent Algernon home after he'd made me lose my temper.

I was wondering whether to slip over to the White Hart. Even with only a few quid staving the wolf from the door a body has a right to drown his sorrows, after Algernon. There was a knock at the door. Funny how you get the feeling. It was Algernon again.

"Forgotten something?" I snapped. I hadn't heard his bike go.

"Er . . . Lovejoy." No stammer, no cheery grin, no move to barge in and start dropping the nearest valuable.

"What is it?"

"Something's wrong," he said quietly. "Your budgies."

I was out and around the side of the cottage before I could think, blundering blindly into my precious camellia. Like a fool I'd not pulled back the curtains for light. I couldn't see a damned thing.

"Fetch a light, Algernon, for Christ's sake!"

"Coming!"

"Manton?" I said softly toward the flight pen. "Wilkie? Are you—?"

The click behind me trapped the garden in light. Algernon's headlamp.

"Mantie?" For a second I could see nothing wrong. I fumbled for the key, thinking to undo the padlock.

Then I noticed the lock's iron loop was wrenched free. The flight's door was aslant and pulled away.

"What is it, Algernon?" I asked, puzzled, stepping forward.

Near my face a small breath sounded. I looked at the door jamb.

Wilkinson was crucified on the wood. Nails were projecting through his blue wings. There was some blood. His feet were drawn upward tight clenched, as if a groping search for a twig on which to rest had been too hopeless anyway.

"A hammer," I babbled. "Pincers. For Christ's *sake*—"

I pushed Algernon aside and crashed through the garden to

my shed, scattering tools and cutting myself in a demented crazy grope along shelves. Things went flying. I tore back, smashing plants and blundering into the cottage wall as I went.

I'd got a claw hammer. It was too short, but it's the only one I have.

"There's not the leverage," I sobbed in a blind rage, trying to get purchase of the claw on the nail. The distance from the nail to the door jamp was too great. I needed some sort of support, some bloody thing to rest the sodding hammer on. Why do I never have the proper fucking tools? I daren't press on his wing. Wilkinson tried to turn his head. I couldn't lodge the hammer against his frail body or it'd crush him.

"Coming, Wilkie," I blubbered. "Coming."

There was nothing for it. I put my thumb under the hammer to protect him and yanked the claw up. My thumb spurted blood. The pain flashed me backward like a blow but the nail was out. Thank Christ. I got up. Wilkinson was hanging by one wing, trying to flap with his bloodstained wing. I held him in my palm to take his weight. I'd forgotten. And I call other people Neanderthal.

"Come here, Algernon." I was suddenly pouring sweat but calm at last. I gave him the hammer in the mad silent glare and nodded at the second nail. My bad hand cupped Wilkinson's body for his own weight. I put my good one over Wilkinson's impaled wing.

"Do it."

"But your hand will—"

"*Do it!*"

He shoved upward. The hammerhead grated smoothly into my knuckles. I heard two bones go. Oddly the pain was less this time though the blood poured in a great stream down my forearm. Wilkinson came free. As he did, he arched his little back. Then he bowed his beak and bit my bloodied thumb as he died. I felt the life go out of him like, well, like a flying bird. It was his last gesture to the world he had known. All that he was or ever had been culminated in one futile bite.

"Hold him, please."

Algernon cupped his gauntlets to receive Wilkinson.

"He's dead, Lovejoy."

"Shut your stupid face," I snarled. "Did you see Manton?"

"No. Maybe he's escaped."

Please God, please. I moved quietly about the flight. "Mantie? Mantie?" Maybe he'd ducked inside his covered house. There was a lot of space where a budgie could hide. Or even get out. I edged toward it, calling softly.

Algernon spotted Manton first. He was hunched on the ground in the corner of the flight, squatted down in the grotesque shadows.

"There!"

"He's safe!" I said. "Manton!" I went over. He didn't move, just stayed facing the flight's open space in that crouching attitude. He'd normally have edged over but was probably stunned at the shock. "Mantie!" I sat on the ground beside him feeling the relief. I was suddenly giddy. I think I'd lost a lot of blood. It seemed everywhere. My hands pulsed pain.

"Lovejoy."

"Yes?"

"I'm afraid I think your other budgie's . . ."

"Algernon," I whispered softly from my position on the grass. "Come here."

He stepped over, still cupping Wilkinson, for all the world like a weird lunar being blocking the headlight's shine.

"Yes?"

"What were you going to say, Algernon?" I asked, still ever so soft and gentle.

I saw his eyes wander nervously behind his specs.

"Er . . . nothing, Lovejoy. Nothing."

"That's good," I whispered. "Now put Wilkinson on his ledge inside."

He moved carefully past carrying Wilkinson in his hands like a priestly offering. A moment later he emerged and stood fidgeting. Everything some people do drives you mad sometimes. Algernon's that kind.

"I've done it."

"Not so loud!" I hissed.

"What will you do now, Lovejoy?" he whispered.

"I'll stay here. He's frightened."

"But he hasn't moved," he said.

"Of course he hasn't," I shot back furiously as loudly as I dared. "He's in a state of shock. Wouldn't you be?" Bloody fool.

"Yes. Of course."

"Then shut your teeth."

"Certainly." He dithered in the oblique light. "What do you want me to do? You're all bleeding."

I was, too, both hands. My left thumb was a pulp. I couldn't move my right hand, which was swelling rapidly. It looked huge, but things always look worse badly lit.

"Shall I get a vet, Lovejoy?" I peered at him suspiciously.

"What would you get a vet for?"

"Er, to tell you . . ." He ground to a halt.

"To tell me what, Algernon?" I whispered savagely.

"Nothing."

"Go home, Algernon." I was suddenly finished.

"Home?"

"Home," I nodded. "Now." I watched him back away toward his motorcycle. It was tilted crazily on the grass. I remember feeling surprised. He's mad about his pop-pop, yet he must have just rushed the machine across the garden and flung it down with the headlamp on.

He pushed it onto the gravel and started up. I heard him call something but that's typical of Algernon, start up a motorbike and assume it's inaudible. Stupid. He slithered down the driveway and out onto the metalled road. Gravel everywhere, of course. Manton and I watched the lights swathe the hedgerows. Finally only the sound remained, faintly humming through the village. We heard him change up, sudden as ever, on the Bercolta road. Then he faded and we were left alone, sitting on the grass in the wretched flight.

The lights of Lexton were shining in the distance, an unpleasing orange. The sky picks up the illuminance and casts a faint tinge on the starglow. I talked to Manton, trying to make him feel that maybe the nightmare was over now and things were at least moving toward normal.

"It's my fault, Mantie," I told him. No use trying to shelve the blame.

He'd normally have chirped there, but it's sensible to harbor your strength if you've had a bad shock, isn't it? You know how it is when you've been ill, how conversation takes it out of you. It's best to stay quiet.

"There's a sensible bird!" I praised still in a whisper. "Keep warm, Mantie."

No good getting one place warm and moving to another, is it? That would be stupid. They know what to do when they're off color. Not like people. We're daft as brushes. Animals are practical. They have an innate sense, haven't they?

*

I don't remember much of the rest. I remember feeling a cold wind springing up, but maybe that was just the effect of the blood loss. I saw blackish gobs and strings of blood on the ground, and all over my leg, and wondered how the hell that had happened. I fell over a few times, mercifully avoiding where Manton huddled. Janie came. I cursed her from habit, and told her to shut the light off.

I remember arguing with her and calling her a stupid, obstinate bitch. She tried bringing an umbrella from the car to shield us from the driving rain which had started up. Good old Algernon had telephoned her. It must have been some conversation.

About dawn I vaguely remember hearing a man's voice asking if this was the one, something like that, and Janie's defiance. I had to pee in situ, which can't have improved my appearance much. The blood on the mud was like those Victorian oil-layered flyleaf bindings. I told Janie to get his seed for him, as he was probably hungry.

I woke in the early light. The rain had ended. No wind. No noise. The robin was looking down at me. I came abruptly out of the nightmare. The robin flew, suddenly sticking like glue to the twig as they do in midflight. I made myself turn and look at Manton. He was crouched because he was impaled on a stake driven into the ground through his little back. Janie was there, a blanket over her dress and almost concealing her mink coat. Stiletto shoes and all. I remembered her husband's voice saying, And people in our position, Janie, and asking, What are you thinking of.

After a bit I told her to help me up. I leaned on her like a drunken matelot, quite unable to see much that wasn't swivelling round and round. She fetched a spade and I dug a hole, alternately yelping and fainting from the excruciating pain and bleeding all down the handle. I wouldn't let her do it. I buried them between the lovely Anne Cocker and a pink grandiflora. Then Janie got me stripped indoors and on the divan for a wash. I was all filth and blood.

"You're in a worse state than China, Lovejoy," Janie called from the alcove.

"Your slang's dated," I gave back. "Gives your age away."

"The doctor will go mad."

"Oh, him," I said.

I wasn't up to repartee. For the first time in the entire business I was aware of the slightly disturbing fact that I was up against a madman. Nichole might be the sweetest woman on earth, but she sure as hell had no control over her tame lunatic.

It was beginning to look as if old Bexon's find was as precious as he'd thought it was.

II

Once upon a time I was a virgin. No, honestly. A bit sweaty and newly hairy, but the real thing. You may remember how it was yourself. I exchanged it for a fob watch. A kindly lady pressed it on me (I mean the watch, folks, the watch) as I left her doorstep, fifteen years old but aged inexpressibly in an hour. She was thirty or so. I couldn't help wondering at the time how someone so obviously senile (over *twenty* whole years of age!) was still managing to get about without a wheelchair, let alone sprint into my big seduction scene with such breathtaking relish. It was a fascinating business and preoccupied me for several hours, after which time I went back for a further lesson. I soon learned her moans were not exactly grief.

Other points also obsessed me. Despite having endured years of teaching to the contrary, I realized that women might actually like males. And I was one of that category. I began watching the sorts of things they did, to see what they really wanted as opposed to what they were supposed to want. I caught on. Women need to be used, to help.

I was up against an arch villain in the form of Edward Rink. I needed help. I looked fondly at Janie as she pottered about, and began to think clearly. It was about time I did.

As Janie got us both ready for bed I watched her every movement. She knew it. They always know when something's on the boil.

Conviction came upon me like an avenging angel. Manton, Wilkinson and Dandy Jack couldn't do anything about Rink. I could. The police would be all puzzled questions and no help. Therefore Bexon's find had to be rediscovered. Not by Edward Rink, but by Lovejoy. That would put the boot into Rink like nothing else on earth. I needed help urgently, until I got my hands back. And I needed money.

"Janie?" I said as she came in beside me that night.

"Yes, love?"

"Look, Janie . . ."

*

Ever noticed how time goes sometimes? You might think it's all the same stuff, day in, day out. It's not. It really does vary. Some minutes leave centuries of wear on you. Others don't age you a second. I'll bet you know the feeling.

That next week was a few eons long. Janie got me the two latest *Time* editions. I usually read that when I can afford it because its punctuation cares. Incidentally, correct grammar's a must for antique manuscript letters and diaries, some of today's soaring valuables. You can allow for spelling mistakes by the milliard, but grammar has to be impeccable. And grammar isn't just using semicolons. If you suspect the genuine old letter which your best friend offers you (". . . actually signed by *her!* On real old-type paper!") could be a forgery, try this test: even if you have no special knowledge of vegetable inks, papers, literary styles or script characteristics, just sit a moment and bother to read it. No cheating, start to finish. Bad grammar or really neffie punctuation should make you think twice, modern education being what it is. This test has saved me more than once. Another tip's the length of sentences. I'm not telling you any more or I'll lose the thread.

Janie got me a recent biography—Queen Mary. I read it, not to see if they mentioned her fabulous collection of jade snuff bottles, but to see if it mentioned how she acquired it. It didn't.

They never do, which really tickles me. Word is that around the British Museum an impending visit from the great lady acted like a tocsin warning of the Visigoths landing. She's rumored to have admired any particular jade piece with such fixed (not to say immovable) admiration that, just to get off the hook, squirming administrators felt compelled to offer her the object. Graciously accepted, of course. I really admire her for that, a collector after my own heart. An example for us all to follow. Of course, it's taking advantage of one's position. But do you know anyone who doesn't? Even God does that.

Janie had the phone reconnected in one day, which must be a record.

"Did you resort to bribery?" I demanded suspiciously.

"They're above that sort of thing," she replied airily, almost as if people ever are. She rang the news around that I'd got flu. Our local quack came and did his nut. People phoned with mediocre deals, all out of my reach. Big Frank nearly infarcted because I was late getting his silvers back. Janie ran them over to the Arcade the first morning to leave them with Margaret.

"We had a little chat," Janie reported back, smug as any woman is after a scrap. I sighed on my sickbed. As if I'd not enough trouble.

Algernon came tiptoeing breathlessly in. The stupid burke brought an enormous bunch of lilies.

"I'm not dead yet, Algernon," I said angrily.

Janie whisked them away diplomatically. Algernon was cheerfully unabashed.

"I've brought you some grapes," he said, "for restorative nourishment."

Janie swifly bundled him outside. I heard him being full of solace in the porch.

"How very sad to witness poor Lovejoy's indefatigable high-spirited pleasantries dampened by such tragic infirmities."

"Quite, Algernon," Janie said firmly. "I'm sorry I can't offer you some coffee, but in the circumstances . . ."

"Absolutely!" he prattled. "On behalf of all of us antiques experts, Janie, may I express gratitude for your *undying* charity in so devotedly sticking to the task of restoring his poor battered physique!"

"Oh, er, well."

One thing. No matter what goes wrong you can always depend on Algernon. I liked the antiques experts bit, may heaven forgive him.

Janie bought food from our village shop, setting tongues wagging. She said nothing to me about there being very little grub in the cottage, but her back had that critical look. I made her write down what she spent and told her I owed it.

Doc Lancaster injected me with some rubbish or other that first day. Janie drove me to the local hospital and they trussed my hands. God, they did hurt.

Janie stayed the first night, jumping a mile at every stray noise. She was terrified and kept asking what sort of maniac would do a thing like that and why.

"We ought to report it," she said more than once.

In the circumstances it was brave of her to stay. The evening of the second night she reported back home in wifely obedience, to check that none of her servants had pinched any of the nineteen bedrooms in her centrally heated mansion. Her husband was throwing a dinner party for business friends and Janie had to baste the carrots.

"Can't stand the pace, eh?" I accused.

"I promised, Lovejoy."

"Remember to crook your little finger over sherry, like posh folks."

She pulled a face and left. Everything I needed was in reach, drinks with straws and all that.

The second day Janie showed me the letter. It had arrived without a stamp. Somebody'd shoved it under the door early.

"I kept it," Janie told me, "because you weren't well enough."

It was mid-morning. I was listening to the radio. One of those staid "experts" was talking about mother-of-pearl decoration— incidentally coming back fast into fashion—and never said the only important thing about it. Keep it covered. Keep it dark. Never, ever put mother-of-pearl under a strong light or on a sunny windowsill. If you do it'll fade, become dull and lifeless. It's practically the only shine we cunning dealers can't restore, imitate properly, or forge. Once it's gone it's gone for good.

This letter.

"I think it's something to do with . . . you know." She opened it for me.

> Dear Lovejoy,
>
> Are you any nearer to handing over the diaries? I sincerely hope that recent events have persuaded you to a wiser course of action than hitherto.
>
> Do not hesitate to contact me should you see sense and wish to sell. Those scribbles can only bring you trouble.
>
> > Yours sincerely,
> > Edward Rink

I looked at Janie, marvelling. "He's mad," I said. "And bloody cool."

"Is he the one that . . . ?" She shivered. I turned the radio off.

"It's evidence," I said, puzzled. "I'll give it to the police. They'll pick him up." Geoffrey, our local bobby, is rumored to wake soon after Easter. Time he did something.

We read the letter again. Janie disagreed with me. "He could mean practically anything."

"He says 'recent events,' " I countered. "It's in his own handwriting."

"That could be anything from the weather to a new offer. You once told me there are a thousand auctions a week. He could say he was talking about a commission."

She was right.

"I'm going to phone him."

"Now, Lovejoy," Janie warned, but I got her to dial the number from his card. We got him third go, a telecommunications miracle.

"Lovejoy? I'm so pleased you rang," the swine said urbanely. "How sensible!"

I tried to hold the receiver lightly but my hand took no notice and hurt itself tightening up.

"Cut it, Rink," I said. "Did you do it?"

"Now, Lovejoy," he purred. "No silliness. I merely want you to be aware your movements are being observed. If you suddenly take it into your head to go anywhere, you'll be spotted. Day or night. More sensible to sell me the diaries and have done."

"What if I've got this conversation on tape?" I asked suddenly.

"You'd be wasting the magistrate's time, Lovejoy." He was laughing, the pig. "I hope you'll see reason. Nichole's desperate."

"No."

He sighed down his end of the blower. "You have one other choice. To become my agent. I would pay you well. And a percentage."

"Why me?" He was off his rocker.

"Because you have the diaries. And the sketch. And I believe you have a peculiar skill where antiques are concerned." He paused. "And that other thing. Poverty."

"I haven't got the sketch."

"Tut tut, Lovejoy. Lies." There was a pause. He cleared his throat, coming to a decision. "Incidentally," he said at last. "I'm sorry about your friend."

"Friend?"

"Dandy Jack." I'd forgotten about him and his accident. "Such a shame. Still, if he lied to Nichole, he deserved—"

I rang off. My hands seemed made of wood. Janie was making coffee. I went shakily back to the divan. Curious, but my head seemed cold and the scalp tight. I let her get on with it for a while before I managed to speak.

"Janie." I saw her back stiffen. "How's Dandy?"

"Mmmm?" She was ever so busy.

"That smelly old geezer from the Arcade. Remember?"

We shared the long horrid silence.

"I couldn't tell you yesterday," she said.

We both watched her assemble my tin coffee gadget. Only Yanks can make coffee properly. They have this knack. I wonder what our women do wrong. I try, but I'm even worse at it than Janie and that's not far from horrendous. It might come out right, we were both thinking, because you never know your luck. The fuse went in the electric plug. She had a high old time unscrewing it and putting it right. We got mixed up over the wires. Well, morons keep changing the colors of the bloody things. It's a wonder we aren't all electrocuted.

"He died early yesterday morning, love. I'm so sorry."

Everything seemed falling to pieces. "Police say anything?"

"Nobody really saw," Janie said. "No witnesses came foreward."

I thought a lot. Dandy suddenly seemed very close. And Manton and Wilkinson. Then fat Henry, and Eleanor. I looked across at Janie. She smiled up, feeling my eyes. We'd a real fire because I'd asked. It was raining. Outside in darkness my robin was probably nodding off. And Crispin my hedgehog was probably roaming, his snuffly infants behind him on the prowl in the muddy grass, filthy beasts. And Tinker Dill, three sheets sloshed in the White Hart by now. And Helen. And Margaret. And Nichole. If you ever bothered to list your responsibilities you'd go spare. I got a pen. Janie saw what I was up to and started us both on separate sheets, copying the diaries. My slowness almost made me bellow with frustration. She was twice as fast. I couldn't do the drawing. Janie had to do that.

It was gone midnight when I phoned Edward Rink to surrender. I wouldn't let him call at the cottage. He gave me a different postal address.

"I give you all I've got of Bexon's," I told him. "You leave my friends alone. Okay?"

"With pleasure," he replied. I swear he was smiling.

We made the diaries into an envelope ready for posting, though it was a homemade job and looked botched.

Janie took it up the lane to our post office as soon as it opened in the morning. By then we'd copied the lot, word for word.

*

For the rest of the day I let my mind rest. I suppose Janie had slipped me a Mickey on Doc Lancaster's orders. Or maybe it was her own brew, the western world's most soporific stimulant. Anyway, I dozed a lot.

By evening I was alert enough to feel certain. Edward Rink was a maniac. He'd killed Dandy Jack. He was determined that, if old Bexon had left a clue about a Roman find, nobody else would get it but him. But what the hell did a beauty like Nichole see in a nerk like that? Doesn't it make you wonder, all those old sayings about women and rich men? Rink must have burgled the Castle to get Bexon's coins from the display case. To check they were genuine Romans, not the crummy electrotypes people are always trying to sell you these days. It was as simple as that. A cool swine. We're never ashamed of our crimes, not really, but being thought inadequate in some way's the absolute humiliation. Aren't people a funny lot?

About eight o'clock our vicar, Reverend Woking, came to ask if I'd sufficiently recovered from my mythical flu to sing in the choir for Dandy Jack. The service would be at ten in a couple of days. They would do the Nelson Mass, though he's not supposed to have papist leanings. I said okay.

"I don't think Lovejoy will be well enough, Reverend," Janie said. "He's had an, er, accident in his workshop."

"Yes, I will," I said. "I'm fine."

"Good, good!" He hesitated, wondering whether to chance his arm and preach to us about Janie's status, but wisely decided to cut his losses.

"Before you start," I put in as Janie prepared to go for me, "you've never heard our tenors. Without me the *Sanctus* is doomed." We bickered this way all evening.

12

Half the church was crowded. Half was bone bare. We were all there. Helen holy without a cigarette. Jimmo with his asbestos cough. Ted the barman from the White Hart. Jill Jenkins with her poodle and a bewildered young uniformed navigator she'd somehow got off a coaster new in harbor that day. Harry Bateman and Jenny lighting candles for all they were worth because their new place opened in the morning. Patrick sobbing into a nasturtium hankie, Lily trying to comfort him and weeping worse. Big Frank from Suffolk trying to look as if he wasn't reading a Sotheby's catalogue of seventeenth-century German and French jewelry. Tinker Dill giving everybody a nasty turn having no cloth cap on and shaming us all to death by stubbing out his fag in our church's exquisite thirteenth-century baptismal font. ("Well, what's the bleeding water in it for, then?" he whispered in an indignant stage bellow when Lily glared.) A miscellany of shuffling barkers unrecognizable with washed heads and clean fingernails—one had even pressed his trousers. Margaret, the only one of us all who knows when to kneel down and which book has the right hymns—we all followed her example. Gimbert's auctioneers had sent a ghoul or two by way of unmitigated grief. And Dig Mason in a morning suit, for God's sake, gear so posh we all knew the Rolls outside was waiting for him and not the coffin. And Algernon falling over twice moving along the pew. He'd brought his uncle, blind Squaddie from the houseboat, who felt the hand-embroidered kneeler a little too long. I'd have to count them after he'd gone. And a few villagers on a day trip from across the road to get a kick out of life.

Oh, and Dandy Jack.

We'd got some flowers in wreaths, one lot shaped like a cross. I'd sold Big Frank my single display Spode plate, cracked and just about in one piece, and bought a lot of flowers. I could tell Janie thought they were the wrong colors but they were bright. Dandy Jack liked bright colors. By then I'd spent up. I got three lengths of wire from a neighbor's lad and threaded the flower stems in and out with green stuff I'd taken from my hedge. It's hard to make a circle. Try it. You don't realize how much skill goes into making things till you do it yourself. It looked just like a real wreath when it was finished. Making it didn't do my hands any good, but I was proud of it. Janie went off somewhere and came back with one of those cards. We wrote "In Remembrance" and our names on it and tied it on with black cotton.

"It looks great, doesn't it?" I asked Janie.

"It's beautiful," she said, which was a relief because Janie can be very critical sometimes. The trouble is I knew she'd have said the same if it hadn't been right. Still.

The coffin was on a bier. I wasn't to carry Dandy because of my hands. Patrick nobly volunteered, but broke down. Trust Patrick. A barker stood in at the last minute. Our church has this small orchestra, five players, counting the organ. Reverend Woking arranging the choir stuck me behind Mary Preston, our plump and attractive cellist. ("You like being here, Lovejoy, don't you?" he said brightly while I avoided Janie's eyes, large in the congregation.)

We didn't sing badly for Dandy Jack. Owd Henry's probably our best bass. He's an eccentric filthy old farmer whose legendary battles with the government over farm subsidies will be sung of by future generations of ecstatic minstrels. It's better than *Beowulf*. He wears an outlandish stovepipe hat for posh, which is hard luck on our altos because as a result they haven't seen a choirmaster's baton beat time since before the war.

Helen never looked up once. She seemed really upset. We listened gravely to Reverend Woking's sermon on Dandy Jack's virtues. It was fifty minutes long, practically par for the course. As far as I could make out it dealt mainly with problems of translating Greek nondeistic pronouns from the Aramaic in the synoptic gospels. Gripping. We'd just got going again when in the middle of it all your friend and mine Edward Rink pottered in, taking my breath away. It was lucky we weren't at the risky bit in the *Agnus Dei,* which is nobody's plaything. Nichole, pale and elegantly fragile, slipped along the pew after him. Algernon kindly passed Rink a hymnal, acknowledged by a curt nod. I'd have to speak to Algernon. Politeness is all very well.

During the service Rink's eyes only met mine once. It was during the *Dies Irae.* That instant any doubts left me. He wouldn't give up, not him. The swine was as cold as any reptile. It was as if I'd gazed into the eyes of the stone crusader on his plinth in our nave. Stone, solid stone. I was so calm I lost concentration for a moment and felt our blacksmith tenor Jim Large's surprised glance along the row. There and then I made my first and last original *De Profundis.* Rink's head was reverently bowed as I prayed, aiming at the middle of his balding spot. That tonsure would have to go. And the scalp as well. I know that a funeral isn't exactly the place to pray for a successful execution, but matters were out of my hands now.

I prayed: Dear Lord, Sorry about this, but Somebody's got to finish Darlin' Edward. And if Somebody doesn't get a move on pretty sharpish, I suppose it'll be up to me. Don't say I didn't warn Somebody in good time. Okay?

The whole lot of us sang a beautiful Amen.

Reverend Woking shook me by suddenly announcing that I would stand and utter a short homily on Dandy Jack. He's a forgetful old sod. He should have said. I could have worked out what to say.

I rose and gazed about. Silence hung. Everybody but Helen was looking.

Dandy Jack was known as Dandy because he was so tatty. He was always cheerful. I remember once he passed over a job lot of two exquisite model railway pieces at an auction. One was a brass miniature of the famous *Columbine* made about 1850 (the one drive-wheel looks a bit big, but don't be discouraged because it always tends to on models). The second was a lovely model of Queen Adelaide's bed coach, No. 2. I've only ever seen their kind once before so they're hardly penny a dozen. When I'd groaned and cursed Dandy for missing a real find, he looked rueful for a second and said, peeved, "I thought they were just bloody toys. What the hell did grown engineers want to make little things like that for?" Then he'd laughed and laughed at his own idiocy, so much that I'd found myself grinning, too. Finally, I gave up being mad and laughed as well. We were in Woody's over egg and chips at the time. Lisa thought us barmy and Woody shouted from the back what the hell was going on in there and if people couldn't behave in a restaurant they'd have to piss off. That only made us worse. The place finished in uproar. Finally we'd gasped our way over to the Marquis of Granby and got paralytic drunk. It's a right game, this.

I looked about. Big Frank was reading his catalogue. Rink was piously bowed. I'm normally quite a good speaker, even with no notice, but it was a bit hard this time. I think I had a cold coming. I tried to start a couple of times but it didn't work. Dandy was almost in arm's reach. The coffin was covered beneath its heaps of flowers by a delicious purple embroidered pall, the precious and delicate *Opus Anglicanum* gold undercouching glittering against the rich color. It's murder to copy. You just try. I recognized it as the one I'd tried to buy off Helen a year before. She'd sent me off with a flea in my ear: "It's for millionaires and the crowned heads of Europe only, Lovejoy." Dandy was neither.

I found myself just looking at the floor in silence. Some woman coughed to fill in, helping out.

"Dandy," I managed at last. "Whatever you find there, be a pal and save some for the rest of us." I paused, thinking of me and Dandy getting ourselves chucked out of Woody's for laughing. It took another minute to get going. Bloody churches are full of drafts. "It's not much help now, Dandy," I said, "but I'll do for the bastard that killed you, whoever he was, so help me." There was a lot of sudden shuffling. I heard Reverend Woking rise suddenly and then sit, aghast. "Goodnight, Dandy," I said. We all fidgeted a bit, coughed ourselves back into action.

That was it. It doesn't seem very much for a whole person.

I'd tell you the rest of the service but there's not much point. Afterward we all went around saying we were sorry. Daft, really. It does no good. It's just what people do, I suppose.

Outside the Reverend Woking was worried sick. He had the harrowed look of a vicar burdened by a debt in search of a debtor.

"Er, Lovejoy—" he said.

"Don't worry. I'll pay for the funeral and the service," I said.

"Oh, fine, fine!" He went back to beaming goodbyes. Isn't religion a wonderful thing?

The rest were already stampeding back to town. Nichole tried to speak to me but her eyes filled up and she turned aside, poor kid. Rink gave me a blank specky stare as they drove past. Yes, I thought, I mean you, you bastard.

Janie stayed with me while they buried Dandy Jack. I told the vicar to get a posh stone for the grave. I'd pay, I said again. Not that it mattered. I'd no money for that either.

"Lovejoy," Reverend Woking intoned in farewell. "Remember that God works in mysterious ways."

I nodded. I accept all that. It's just that I wish the Almighty had a better record in social reform.

I walked home.

*

Janie told me there was a man watching the cottage. I'd seen him on the wooden seat outside the chapel when I went to the village shop.

"He comes sometimes and sits on the ruined gate by the copse," she reported.

"Any special time?"

"Morning and evening."

I went up the lane and accosted him late on the third day. He was rather apologetic about it all, a pleasant bloke, about twenty-five.

"I hope you don't mind," he said, embarrassed.

"Are you from Janie's husband?" I tried to snarl like I do at Algernon but couldn't.

"No. I've tried to keep—" he thought a moment, then brought out with pride—"a *low profile*." He smiled anxiously.

"Are you supposed to be a . . . private eye?" We were both using words nicked from those corny detective series on telly.

"I *am* one," he said defiantly, actually believing it.

I looked at him with interest. He was the first I'd ever seen.

"We never get them hereabouts." We were as embarrassed as each other. "Who employs you?"

"I can't tell." He was going to die at the stake for his profession. What a pathetic mess.

"Rink?" I said, and he quickly looked away. "Thank you. That's what I want to know. Don't catch cold."

So it was Rink. That gave me time. I must have read both diaries a hundred times that week but I'd learned nothing. Rink must be in the same boat as I was. Reading them over and over would have been as dull as ditchwater if it hadn't been for Dandy Jack and that other business in my garden.

"He's just an ordinary bloke," I reported to Janie. "I thought they were all hard as nails, as in Chandler."

"How horrid. What will he do?"

"Oh, wait till I set off for the Isle of Man and phone Rink." I shrugged. "Then they'll follow me, I suppose."

"Are you going after all?" she asked.

I gave her my very best and purest stare.

"Of *course* I'm not," I said. "I only meant if."

13

The third day I burned the flight. I know how the Vikings felt. An end, a beginning. I used paraffin to get it going and stood back. My cherry tree got a branch singed, but then living's just one risk after another, isn't it? A neighbor came running down the lane to see if the sky was falling. He breeds those long flat dogs which bark on middle F. I reassured him. He left after giving my wrapped hands a prolonged stare.

I waited for Janie. She arrived about teatime.

"Can I . . . have some money, Janie?" I watched her turn from hanging her coat up. I've only three pegs behind the hall door. I'd sold the mahogany stand that morning through Tinker Dill. That's Janie's best character point—never asks where things have suddenly gone. She may not care for my behavior very much, but she accepts that it goes on. I think she tolerates me like a sort of personal bad weather, changeable but just something that has to be endured.

"Yes, love."

"I'll pay it back. Soon."

"How much?" She fumbled in her bag. "Will a check do?"

"Yes, please. Just enough for a couple of weeks." I had to say sorry, after refusing all this time, but she said men were stupid sometimes and what were bits of paper. I'd have agreed if she meant compared with antiques.

"Keep it," she said.

"No, no," I said. "A thousand times, no." You have to be patient. She called me silly and got all exasperated. I think women have very simple minds.

I looked at the check. Funny that a small strip of marked paper can mean so many antiques. When you think.

"It's beautiful." That must have been me speaking. I took it reverently off the table. "What are you laughing for?"

"Oh, shut up, Lovejoy." She turned away. It didn't sound like laughing.

"I love you," I said to her. She laughed and faced me, wobbling. Her cheeks were a bit wet.

"Lovejoy, you're preposterous!"

"Eh?"

"You get everything wrong" she said, subsiding somewhat and smiling out of character. "It's the other way around. *I* love *you*."

"That's what I said." I was puzzled. Just when things seemed on the mend between us. Women surprise me sometimes.

"Come here to me," she said, smiling properly now.

"Just a minute." I found a pen and paper to make a list, but Janie took the paper away. My hands were too clumsy to argue.

"Shut up, Lovejoy," she said, "for heaven's sake." So I did.

*

An hour later I woke from the post-loving doze. My mind instantly thought of what I should do.

Friend Rink had money. He could afford a watcher. All he had to do was wait. And if I ever made a dash for the Isle of Man he could either fly ahead or send his watcher to keep track. But nobody can move without money, and my income from Squaddie barely kept me alive. Janie's money was only for starters. I'd need more. I didn't know how long the search would take. Suddenly Janie was watching me, worried. She cheered up when I said I needed her help.

"With some antiques?"

"Yes. Cleaning and improving them."

"For selling?"

"You're learning."

A mischievous smile lit her face.

"Lovejoy. You . . . really need *my* help? Not Algernon's?"

"Especially not Algernon's."

"Nor Margaret's?"

"Good heavens, no." I wanted no dealers.

"But I know nothing about antiques."

Careless old Lovejoy almost said that was the point, but I covered up quickly by telling her I trusted her.

"More than your friends?" she pressed. "More even than Helen?" Typical.

"Much more," I said. Honesty was everywhere. I felt quite moved myself.

"Then I will. On one condition."

"Eh?"

"That you pay me, Lovejoy."

"Pay?" I yelped, starting upright in the bed. "What the hell with?"

"Give me one day—of your time." She was adamant. I'd have to go carefully. What a dirty trick.

"One day?" I countered uneasily. "You can have tomorrow. That do?"

She shook her head prettily. She's always attractive when she's up to no good. Sometimes I think women play on our feelings.

"No. When I say. For *me* to decide what we do for a change."

"But what if—?"

"No deal if you're going to make excuses, Lovejoy. Get somebody else." I thought hard and with cunning but there seemed no way out.

"Well, it's a bit unfair," I said reluctantly. "Will you give me some notice?"

She hugged me, delighted.

"Possibly, Lovejoy," she said. "And possibly not." I tried wheedling but got no further. She told me, smiling sweetly, "All we have is time." She fluttered her eyelashes exaggeratedly. I thought of the forthcoming death of Edward Rink, Esq., and smiled, in control.

*

Now here comes the bit I said you wouldn't like. Same as your grandma's beef tea, it won't be pleasant but it will do you good.

If you're poor it will save you a few quid. If you're one of the struggling rich it may save you millions.

*

All I've said so far about antiques is right *for antiques*. But think a second. What exactly is "an antique"? Look at the articles around you. We can agree on many items, for a start. Your teacup made last week in good old Stoke-on-Trent isn't antique, for example. And that ball-point pen made last year isn't either. Right. But those three decorative coronation mugs on your mantelpiece, how about them? Well, Liz II hardly qualifies. And that George VI cup? Not really. That George V mug, then? Sorry, no. Notice how difficult it's getting. None of these is "an antique," not truly. Some people define "antique" as being one hundred years from today. Others claim twenty-five years is plenty. And there's some logic in that, I suppose. After all, jubilees begin at twenty-five years, and a century's the magic hundred, isn't it? But the actual honest truth's sadly different. Anything from now to twenty-five years ago is *modern*. Going back from then to a century ago's *bygone*. Then there's a bit of a twilight zone. *Then* come antiques.

Antiques begin, fans, in the shoulder of that lovely blissful Year of Grace 1836. No matter what dealer groups do with fanciful definitions keep that magic date in mind. But please don't think I'm advising you to sprint out and hurl your Coronation souvenirs into the nearest jumble sale. That would be foolish, because three other factors besides age come into it. They're *rarity, nature* and *condition*.

And here it comes, pals, the end of our beautiful friendship. What I've just told you is okay for antiques as such. It's known by any dealer worth a light, and by most collectors with any sense. But nobody knows it like forgers do.

*

You reach antiques by standing on piles of money. So my mind went: One, I need money. Two, I therefore need to sell antiques. Three, I have no antiques. Four, I therefore need to sell some things that resemble antiques but which aren't the real thing. Hey ho.

105

14

Before I go on, don't knock forgery. It's a respectable trade and has done a lot of good for mankind. Anyway, what's wrong with a good honest forgery? People only hate the idea because it means they can't afford to be lazy when buying. Michelangelo started out as the most expert forger of the Renaissance, copying an ancient sketch so well even his teacher Ghirlandaio was misled, mainly because Michelangelo had cleverly aged it. And even then he didn't own up, only being caught out by being overheard bragging about it in the boozer. And he went from strength to strength. It's a sobering thought that he would never have got himself launched, had it not been for his famous Sleeping Cupid forgery—he buried the statue where it would be found, and saw it actually sold to the famous collector Cardinal Riario. He'd the sense to include a "straightener" (a giveaway) so he could claim his just deserts later on.

So, folks, an expert may *do* the actual forging, but it's us that make it something it never was in the first place.

Ever since I can remember I've been making. As a kid I'd only to hear how William Blake revived and modified Castiglione's monotype engraving for me to go thieving copper sheet and working dementedly till all hours to see how it could have been done. It might sound odd behavior, but it's taught me more about antiques than any other experience—and I include reading. I've tried everything: casting bronzes, silversmithing, hammering coins, early "chemical" photogravure, wood-block printing, making flintlocks, copying early German clocks, making parchment like St. Cuthbert's monks in his Lindisfarne outfit, ironwork, Chinese glazes, making chain armor, anything.

I often think of Fabergé, that great (permit me to repeat that, folks: great) designer. He didn't actually make his brilliant masterpieces: that beavering was all done by subterranean troglodytic minions in his workship, such as Durofeev, the self-taught mechanic of St. Petersburg who made the fabulous gold peacock which still trots out of the exquisite rock crystal Easter egg Fabergé gave to the Czar. When the new bureaucracy poured into his Moscow business at the Revolution's takeover, Fabergé simply begged leave to don his coat and hat and politely fade out of this modern era. The coming of the Admin. Man was just too much. Understandable, perhaps, My reaction's different. I fight. The opponent is barbarism.

Being an antiques man and not having much else to fight with, I fight with antiques. And now I had a fight on my hands.

    *

I explained to Janie I had work to do.

"More of that mysterious business in the cottage you won't let me see?" she complained.

"That's it."

"If I find it turns out to be a secret cupboard containing a dumb blonde, Lovejoy—"

"Very funny," I got back, not wanting her to think of hiding places. "Your husband's back today, anyhow. Time for your homework."

"There's an alternative course of action." Janie never smiles in this sort of conversation.

"Tell any dealers you see I'm still contagious and they're not to call." I pushed her out. I could tell that pleased her. She didn't even say "Including Margaret?"

"Phone me," she said.

"Yes," I promised. She'd written the best times down in case some stray serf picked up the blower and summoned her better half to take me to task. I stood at the door watching her drive off in the Lagonda. Like a mobile Stately Home.

*

My workshop's only a shed. As much as possible I like the scene to be set correctly. No electricity. No gas. No lasers or power drills, just candles and an oil lamp. I have one wooden bench, marble slab for special work and an old dental drill, foot-pedalled to a horizontal spindle for grinding and polishing. At the back of the garage there's a small brick kiln I built and some leather foot-bellows I made. That's really it.

The law on forgery's a bit funny, as on everything else. Anyone's allowed to make likenesses without infringing copyright law. But if you pass one off as somebody else's work, for gain, the magistrates get cross and you're for it. So, sign any fake you've made *with your own name,* however skillfully hidden, and you're in the clear.

I decided that Beck was the mark. For him I decided to make a special effort. I would skate very close to the edge. Beck unsuspectingly would provide the money. I would knowingly provide the forgeries, and I'd stay legal.

I'd already tried copying Roman and Egyptian glass. One heats the glass—pick modern glass tubing because it's so easy to melt and get going. The idea is to get a blob of glass on the blowpipe, fairly centrally. Then push it into a mold you've made ready, of earthenware, sand or whatever. Blow like hell and keep the pressure up until you're practically on your knees. Then simply cut the glass off with a big pair of shears. Whatever impressions or patterns you've made to decorate the mold's inner surface, that's the pattern you'll have on your little glass bottle. Okay?

Well, no, not really. The weight and density of the glass will give you away—ancient glass seems so light. And the colors (green, yellowish, blue). So add some color from mineral compounds when the glass is in the molten state. Trial and error's the only thing here, I'm afraid.

It took me a day to make three. One was a bowl, another a small jug and the last a small bottle. I did one extra by the lost-sand process because it was probably the first-ever of all processes mankind found. My own method is to sink a weighted earthenware bowl into a crucible and let the crucible cool, probably how it was done in Phoenician times.

I engraved LOVEJOY FECIT, my address and the day's date in minute stippled lettering as deep inside as I could reach. A buyer wouldn't look with a hand lens. I was really proud. They looked more Roman than the Roman stuff. Or did I mean Egyptian?

I next did a découpage, from an old—last year's—Christmas card. This was for speed, though my hands made it a painfully slow business. Profits are not enormous, but you can knock out a few quid by forging your first "antique" as follows: find a ruined wardrobe, table, anything on its last legs, say your auntie's worm-pocked cupboard. Make sure it's not antique. Take the back off. Old, dried, wrinkled, warped wood, right? Cut a piece about thirteen inches by nine. Now go to that heap of Christmas cards you keep meaning to chuck out. Find one picture print you think looks oldish. Peel the design—perhaps flowers and grasses—off the thick card, and glue it to the wood, which you'll have by now sandpapered smooth and wiped clean. Leave it a day. Scrape some burnt umber from your nephew's paint set onto your finger, and rub it into the *edges* of the stuck design. Not too much. Warm it all in a fireplace. Then varnish the lot, several coats. Use the new synthetic varnish if you like, with maybe a scratch of chrome yellow to the final coat. Rose madder does quite well, too, but you'll need to be very careful with that. And there's your genuine William IV, or even late Georgian, decorated place mat ("from the house of a local country squire," as we dealers would say). Never mind that Georgian country squires practically never used table mats. You have the money for your next meal.

Then I did a lovely tiling job. A tiler is a low quality forged painting, a sort of a beginner's forgery, though with an impressive record of giddy success. It's done like this: take a modern book showing the paintings by, say Samuel Palmer. You take one area of a picture (say, a mid-ground forest) and trace its outline on a paper. Then you trace a barn from a second painting, the mountain from a third, sky from a fourth and so on. If you don't care about the book you cut the pictures out, and assemble the paper bits, very like a jigsaw or tiling on a wall, until your blank paper is filled. Then, with any old watercolor paintbox, you assemble the painting. Tip: do it fast. You'd be astonished at the speed real forgers work. I suspect the original masters worked just as fast. Think for example of the contemporary descriptions of Turner. He always had his skates on.

For Beck's "Palmer" I used the heaviest paper I could find, which was about 120 poundage. Heavy paper always helps. It took about an hour. Then, ensuring I'd a lovely straightener—my name in pencil, done minutely in a crease folded into the area to be covered by the frame—I blew a faint gust of soot and heated soil-dust over it. Never use soot alone. I fronted it with faintly brown-tinted glass. (Well, actually, I couldn't afford that, so I inserted a sheet of thin plastic over which I'd washed a mixture of Vandyke brown and chrome yellow.) Any trick for age's sake, forgers say.

*

Next was a copy of a letter, copied from a famous book of Peninsular War letters, ostensibly from one of Wellington's soldiers at Salamanca. I used ordinary typing paper, two sheets glued together to get that crackle and frayed with a wire brush. I wrote using a real quill and some ink made from crushed oak-galls out of the garden. Two or three very warm warmings in the oven, and my own name in a grand convoluted signature so complex even I had to trace the scrolled lines to read it.

I invented my own antique musical instrument next. Vaseline smeared over an old bike inner tube, cut and clipped to be one long inflated rubber. Two inner cardboards from lavatory rolls, also Vaselined, and a handful of four-inch glue-soaked bandages rolled around the tube and the cardboards and waggled into a double-S shape. Once they'd set, I pricked the inner tube and pulled it out as it deflated. The rigid S-shaped piece was now solid enough to wind more glue-soaked bandages around. When it hardens you can cut oval holes at various distances along it. I drilled a piece of horn into a mouthpiece shape and stuck it in the thin end. The trouble is that bandages are white so I stained the thing with tea bags crammed into a jam jar with a little burnt umber and saffron powder before varnishing. I engraved my signature, the date and my address around the inner rim of the mouthpiece and the belled rim. LOVEJOY FECIT again. Ten to one Beck would call it a crumhorn without knowing a crumhorn from a foghorn. A million to one he'd never look for the maker's name. I baked it gently in a low oven.

They looked really good. I'll have to be careful what I buy in the future, I thought. I lined them up on my bench for a last look. Good. Or, rather, bad. I normally only do things properly to teach myself. But this was different. Once people start going about killing people, people have to take very special measures against certain people, don't people? Even if it means people taking frightful risks.

I was ready.

*

That evening I took out my one precious piece, very dear to me. A jade coin, apparently from the Ch'ien Lung period. I had it in my priest-hole. Now the cupboard was bare.

I phoned Tinker Dill at the White Hart. He called at the cottage for the jade. I told him to enter it at Gimbert's auction by a devious route and under a fictitious name. He was going to ask what it was all about but looked at my face.

"Will you be there, Lovejoy?" he asked.

"Oh, yes," I said. "Wouldn't miss an auction for the world." I gave him the busfare back to town. "I'll be in action again soon, Tinker."

"See you, then."

"Oh, Tinker," I called after him. "See that Beck's there, can you?"

He grinned. "Thought as much." He waved from the drive. I saw him hitch a lift from the milk float further up the lane.

Ready, steady, go.

15

The day of the auction dawned blue and clear. By six o'clock I was up and sweating like a dog, nervous and on edge. I went about trembling and singing, clattering the pots and getting ready twice. I'm always like this. Janie was due to come for me at nine-fifteen. By then I was a wreck. The wildlife got their breakfast three times over and I lost pounds. I couldn't eat any breakfast though I'd got some of those flaky things out and made some toast.

"There must be easier ways to earn a living, Lovejoy." Janie pulled the Lagonda in and sat staring at me.

"Why are you so bloody late?" I couldn't unlock the car door for fumbling.

"I'd like to point out that I'm early," she said sweetly. "And good morning, world."

"Well, then," I said lamely.

"And it isn't locked."

Two down. I got in sheepishly and we left the village sedately, a visiting lady and her agent respectably bound for an ordinary sale. I always feel so sick at this stage. The first sight of town by the nursery gardens makes me retch. That's the trouble with ordinary sales—there's no such thing. Every single one's a matter of life and death.

"Are you all right, darling?" Janie slowed at the station. "Shall I stop?"

"No." I'd only have to get out and run.

"If I see something I like in the auction can I get it?"

"Tell me." It took me three tries to speak. My mouth was sand. "And I'll tell you what to do."

"Oh, I can bid," she said, poor little innocent. "I know how." The eternal cry.

"Everybody knows *how* about everything," I said. "Only Caesars and Wellingtons know *when*."

She shrugged. "Anyway, there may be nothing nice there," she countered. "And keep your hand off my knee when I'm driving, Lovejoy."

"Oh, sorry." My hand had actually fallen on her knee again. My mind was on other things.

*

No matter what the auction is, somewhere deep in that crush of old mangles, derelict bikes and discarded trinkets is a gem, a real trophy going for a song.

I've never yet been to an auction where every single thing's rubbish. I don't deny that on viewing day you'll hear plenty of people all about you saying disgustedly, "Did you ever see such rubbish?" Have you ever wondered why? If you'd spotted, say, the missing chunk of the Cullinan Diamond thinly disguised as a paperweight between a battered radio and a heap of gardening tools, what else would you do but go about pretending everything was a waste of time? I mean, you don't want all Hatton Garden clattering in. So naturally you go about saying it's all a heap of dross. Loudly. Often. We call it "shading" the stock. It puts honest people (me, maybe you) off. You'd be surprised how effective it is. You'd also be astonished at seeing how many of these doom-gospellers actually turn up on sale days all eager to bid for the same rubbish they've previously decried.

Janie put the Lagonda in Gimbert's yard with the dealers' old bangers. We left it looking like a cathedral among kennels. We walked down the hill, Janie primly keeping her distance from me and smiling good mornings to one and all. We were all assembling. Barkers tend to huddle in doorways, smoking and nodding. A housewife who will be bidding usually stands waiting vigilantly in one spot, presumably in case Sotheby's suddenly sends a dozen experts to bid for the ashtray she fancies.

It's a saying around here that the best trees are found in forests, and they're very hard to tell from all the rest. When you go bidding just remember that people aren't what they say or think or seem. We're all what we *do*.

*

There were already eighty or so people in. Everybody was on tenterhooks, hearts thumping and fingers itching. I had to tell Janie about her coat. She had unconsciously adopted the old shoplifter's trick of carrying her coat over her arm.

"Do you mean they'd think me a—thief?" She was outraged.

"No, love. Er," I invented, "you *remind* them, that's all." It had to do, though she was deeply riled. The dealers relaxed as she slipped the coat over her shoulders.

This morning Gimbert's auction warehouse was offering several hundred items of assorted junk ranging from battered old tables to tatty trinkets in those pathetic little boxes signifying recent bereavements and relatives desperate to clear out. Some people say all life's only must, dust and rust. People wandered about among the bicycles and lawnmowers, mostly without any idea. From the entrance it was ugly, dowdy, pretty rough. To me, exquisite. Somewhere in all that rubbish was that missing Leonardo. I would find it or get damned close. To some that single bargain would be nothing more than a ring, a worn Edwardian matchbox, a Victorian maid's mobcap. To me, a delight as spectacular as the crown jewels.

There's a technique. You *drift*. Don't tear in thinking to see it all and race on to the next auction. Don't search. Idle about. After an hour or so a gradual change takes place. Objects begin to move like swallows shuffling on a wire. I swear it. You can feel it, even see it. Dusty old items you wouldn't look at twice shift into prominence as if they somehow grow taller and beckon stealthily. But take no notice yet, just carry on drifting. In time one will be practically shrieking for your attention. That grotty old desk covered with rubbish will have grown to twice its size and be throbbing like an old cinema organ. Everything else will fade into the background. And of course it will turn out to be a genuine early New England block-fronted desk, so ugly yet so much desired today. On a good day maybe two or even three items call you. Once I even had to mortgage my cottage again to pay for the seven delicious pieces I'd bought.

Smiling with anticipation I drifted in.

Gimbert's is two enormous galleries half-roofed in glass so the shadows confuse the innocent. Light's the auctioneer's worst enemy. It isn't bad as auction halls go, but you have to watch it. Ringers turn up once a month. They're easy to spot, shuffling about, looking at customers and nowhere else the way they do. They *have* to, in case a serious collector turns up. If one does, he spells trouble—the collector may be willing to pay an antique's true worth and ringers aren't. They pretend to ignore the desired object, except for one ringer who bids. After the auction they'll meet in some bar and auction the antique among themselves, sharing the net gain.

It's illegal.

"Morning, Lovejoy." Dear old Beck. Fancy that.

"Morning."

"On the borrow?" he asked, grinning. "Or selling that Isen?"

He'd fished me more than once, knowing I can't help going after antiques. You fish friends—or, indeed, enemies—by telling them, say, a genuine painting by Isen (Kano Eishin) is somewhere or other, making it up. Well, who in their right mind can resist Isen's luscious white highlighted robes and his gusting winds driving those painted ships? Naturally one hares off after it. For somebody like Beck it's a joke. For somebody like me, going without grub to raise the fare on a wild goose chase, it's no giggle.

"Sold it," I said back coolly. He stared. "Thanks for the tip, Beckie." That shut him up.

I drifted on, nodding and passing the occasional word. A mote spoon donged for attention from among a mass of crud in a crammed cutlery drawer. I'm always astonished people's heads don't swivel at the sudden clanging. The trouble is that genuine antiques make your breathing funny. I went over casually and pretended to examine the kitchen cabinet. Mote spoons are often forged, but this was true 1752 or so. No maker's mark. Odd long pointed handle and a fenestrated bowl.

Lily and Patrick arrived to look at the phoney tapestries and Big Frank lumbered in to maul the silver. Delmer came flashily in, staggering under the weight of his gold rings. Even before he was through the door those of us who knew him glanced about to see where the books were heaped and stepped out of the way because he's a fast mover. I like dealers like Delmer. Only books. He'd walk past a Rubens crucifixion painting to bid for a paperback. Sure enough he streaked for the corner, slamming a nice pair of Suffolk chairs aside on the way. I sighed. It takes all sorts, but God alone knows why.

"Anything, Lovejoy?" Tinker Dill, an unnerving sight this early, obediently emerging from the mob on time. This was my cue. I hoped Tinker could remember his lines.

"Not really, Tinker." I made sure I said it wrong enough for alert friends to notice.

"I'll slide off, then."

"Er, no, Tinker." A lot of ears pricked. "Hang about."

"Lovejoy wants you to bid for that drawerful of old knives and forks, Tinker." Beck again.

"Right," I said angrily. I didn't have to act. Beck really does rile me. "Get it, Tinker."

"It looks a right load of rubbish, Lovejoy—" Tinker, badly overacting.

"*Get it*, Tinker."

"Lost your wool?" Beck said innocently. "Just because I got that Burne-Jones sketch? Sold it yesterday, incidentally. To your friend, businessman with the blonde." So Rink had traced it successfully after all. I hadn't time to worry about the implications for the minute.

"Look, Lovejoy—"

"Do as you're bloody well told, Tinker."

I pushed off through the crowd, pretending to be blazing.

116

"Easy, Lovejoy." Lennie offering me a fag. I shook my head irritably. I deserved an Oscar.

"Those bloody trawlies get to me, Lennie."

"Jill said she'd be in with that opal photo."

"Thanks." Photographs were once done on opal glass and colored by watercolors. She was asking the earth, naturally.

I drifted. Delmer had found a copy of *The History of Little Goody Two-Shoes* and looked as pleased as Punch. Don't laugh. The public's soaked up over two hundred editions since 1765.

"Is it one of Newberry's?" I couldn't help muttering the vital question as I drifted past. He dropped it casually back into the job lot and sauntered off, shaking his head absently. A good dealer's a careful one. I touched it for the clang and drifted in the opposite direction. The unique copy's in the British Museum, but Newberry turned them out for donkeys' years in St. Paul's Churchyard during Georgian times so they're still knocking about. I had a brief look at the rest. Delmer would have spotted the first edition of Ransome's *Swallows and Amazons* which lay among a pile of gramophone records, so no chance there.

I drifted some more. The crowd collected. Ringers were there, trimmers, hailers, tackers, lifters, nobbers, screwers, backers and sharpers, a real tribe of hunters if ever there was one. I can't help smiling. I actually honestly like us all. At least we're predictable and therefore reliable, which makes us a great deal more preferable than the good old innocent public. Some people were gazing in the window at us. Well, if you stay out of the water at least the sharks can't get you.

The jade coin was in the corner case, numbered seventy. By the time the auctioneer banged us to the starting gate practically everybody in the room was pretending to ignore it.

"Lot One," he piped, a callow youth on his tenth auction. "A very desirable clean modern birdcage complete with stand. Who'll bid?"

"Dad send you to feed the crocodiles, sonny?" one of the Aldgate circus called. Laughter.

A woman near me tutted. "How rude!" she exclaimed. I nodded sadly.

"Modern manners," I said. She approved of my sentiments and I was glad. I'd seen her inspecting the kitchen cabinet, and Tinker Dill was on to it, with my money.

Sharks and cutthroats, we all settled and paid rapt attention to the sale of a birdcage.

*

I watched it come. Ten, Twenty. At Thirty-two Margaret bid for and got a pair of small Lowestoft soft, paste porcelain animal figures, a swan and a dog. I don't like them much because of the enamelling but I was glad for Margaret. Delmer got his *Goody Two-Shoes* and a pile of others for a few pence at Thirty-eight. At Forty Tinker Dill got the cabinet, though Beck had a few laughs at my expense and threatened loudly to compete in the bidding. One of the Birmingham lads wandered over curiously during the bidding to look at the cabinet, but by then Tinker had guessed right and was standing idly by, leaning against the drawer where the mote spoon was. My mote spoon now. The Brummie stared across at me carefully. I smiled benevolently back. I saw him start edging across to the others of the Brummie circus. Well, they're not all daft.

Harry Bateman tried a few bids for a Victorian copy of an anonymous Flemish school oil and failed. Why first-class nine-teenth-century artists wasted their talents making copies of tenth-rate seventeenth-century paintings I'll never know, but you couldn't say this to Harry.

"Lot Seventy," the auctioneer intoned.

This was it. My jade piece, a dark lustrous green with brown flecks and one oblique growth fault, was carved in the form of an ancient Chinese cash coin. Jade is the wonder stone, matt and oily and soft to look at yet incredibly hard. It can resist shock blows time after time. (Remember that those large but thin uninteresting jade rectangles you see are most probably nothing less than temple *bells,* to be struck when tuning string instruments. Very desirable. A complete set is worth . . . well, a year's holiday. Give me first offer.) I saw Beck glance around. The bidding started. I went in quick, too quick for some. Jimmo was prominent in the early stages. Then Jonas came in, raising in

double steps to the auctioneer's ecstasy. Jonas is a youngish retired officer with money, no knowledge and determination. This
combination's usually at least fatal, but Jonas has survived in the
business simply by refusing to give up. From an initial dislike
his fellow dealers, me included, switched to neutrality and finally with reluctance to a sort of grudging acceptance. He's silver and pre-Victorian book bindings with occasional manuscripts thrown in for luck. Lily was there but left the bidding
when I started up. Patrick looked peevish when she stalled—
there'd be trouble over her tea and crumpets when he got her
home. Four others showed early and chucked up. That left me,
Jonas, a Brummie and Beck. I bid by nodding. Some people bid
by waving programs or raising eyebrows. Remember there's no
need to wave and tell everybody who's bidding. Don't be afraid
your bid will be missed. A creased forehead is like a flag day to
an auctioneer. He gets a percentage.

On we went, me sweating as always. I was beaten when Beck
upped. Jonas must have sensed something wasn't quite right, because he hung on only briefly, then folded. I saw that the Brummie bidder was the one who'd crossed to look at the kitchen
cabinet. He finally stopped when Beck showed the first sign of
wavering, clever lad. The jade was knocked down to Beck.

Beck glanced triumphantly in my direction through the
throng. I glared back. He would brag all year how he picked up
his rare ancient Chinese jade coin in the face of organized local
opposition.

"He had us, Lovejoy," Jonas said, pushing past at the break. I
followed him muttering to the tea bar.

"Hard luck, Lovejoy," from Jimmo. "Hell of a price."

"Outsider!" I heard Patrick snapping at Beck.

"Things are getting worse every day," I agreed.

Janie had our teas waiting in the brawl. We had to fight our
way into a corner to breathe. Tinker kept Janie a part of a bench.
I kissed her.

"Watch out, Lovejoy," she said, smiling brightly to show ea-
gle-eyed watchers we were only good friends. "One of my
neighbors is here." She flashed a brilliant grimace toward a vigilant fat lady steaming past. "I'm sorry, love," she added, moving

primly away from my hand which had accidentally alighted on her knee.

"What about?"

"The old jade." She reproved me under her breath, "I'd have given you some money. Nobody need have noticed."

"Why?"

"Then you could have got the jade instead."

"Oh. Thanks, love," I said bravely. "You get these disappointments."

She eyed me shrewdly. "Didn't you want it, Lovejoy?"

"Of course I did," I lied evenly. "I always want ancient Chinese jade, don't I?"

She kept her eyes on me. "Then why are you so pleased, Lovejoy?"

"Oh, just life in general."

"Was there something wrong with it?"

"Certainly not!" I said indignantly.

I ought to know. It had taken me nine weeks to make, nine weeks of pure downright slavery over my old pedalled spindle. It was absolutely perfect. Authentic in every detail, except for the small point that it was a forgery.

Now calm down, gentle reader. Can I be held responsible if some goon buys a piece of jade—it really was jade, which is mined nowadays in Burma, New Zealand and Guatemala—without examining it? And if you're still wondering why I bid for a forgery I'd made and put up for auction myself, take my tip: please feel free to read on, but don't ever go into the antique game. My name and address I'd scratched in minute letters around the margins of the inside hole, date included. If customers don't look with a hand lens, it's just tough luck, and the more fools they. I couldn't exactly put my name in neon lights on a thing the size of a dollar, could I? It would spoil the effect.

"Lovejoy." She had that odd look.

"I didn't touch your knee," I said indignantly.

"What are you up to?"

I was narked with Janie. Right in the middle of a chattering mob of customers in an ordinary small-town auction she starts suspecting me of being up to some trickery. Women can be very

120

suspicious of fundamentally good honest motives. It's not very nice. I really do believe they have rather sinister minds. Where there's no reason to be suspicious they suddenly assume you can't be trusted. I find it very unsettling. They're the ones who're always on about trust, then they go and show they've got none themselves. It's basically a sign of poor character.

At Lot Two-Eighty I crossed to Tinker. The crowd thinned. In the smoke the substitute auctioneer, a hoary old veteran who wasn't letting us get away with anything, droned cynically on. We had space to pretend interest. Tinker made a great show of pulling out the drawer and complaining about the uselessness of the buy I'd made. The auctioneer called for quiet, please, during the bidding. I slipped the mote spoon into my pocket and relaxed.

"Put the rest back in next week's auction, Lovejoy?" Tinker asked. This is all quite legal.

"Yes." I made sure we weren't overheard. "Grumble a lot while you do."

"I'll try."

I had to stop myself from a wide grin at Tinker's crack. Barkers can out-grumble the most miserable farmer.

Janie went to have her hair done. We eventually met at a coffee garden near the river walk, a short distance away. I'd tried to get her to come to Woody's but she wouldn't. I said I could return her the money she'd lent me. She said don't be silly.

We talked on the way back to Gimbert's, where the auction was practically over. I caught sight of Beck and said so-long to Janie. They were in the auction yard among starting cars and people hauling various lots out of the covered part. A woman was asking how to get an enormous cupboard home. Time to haul in the net.

"Look, Beck," I said. He stopped bragging to his mates. "About that jade."

"Want it, Lovejoy? It's for sale." There was a roar of laughter, my expense.

"I've a couple of things you might swap."

"Good stuff?"

"Two are."

"What kind of stuff?"

"Good stuff," I said cagily.

"Where?"

"My place."

He thought a moment. Finally he trod his cigarette.

"I'll come."

I got a taxi. In the ride out to the village he showed me the jade.

"Lovely piece of work, eh?"

I could hardly disagree. At the cottage he insisted that the taxi wait.

I had the pieces distributed around the living room. It wouldn't do to show him the workshop.

"This glass jug," I told him. He reached for it. "I've this bowl as well."

"Both yours?" he asked warily. I nodded. "Honestly? Roman or Egyptian?"

His eyes were everywhere while I busied myself getting a glass of beer. I had to steady my hands, back turned toward him, while I poured, in case the glass clinked and gave away my anxiety. It's a right bloody game, this. When I gave him the drink I could see he'd noticed my tiler, hung prettily on the wall. And my nonmusical instrument casually placed over the fireplace.

"You've one or two things here, Lovejoy," he said.

"I don't want to sell."

"No?" He looked shrewdly about. "This place looks pretty bare. And where's your car? You used to have one."

"Well, I had to sell it."

"I see." He sat examining the glass bowl and jug I'd made. "Good Roman," he pronounced. I said nothing. "Cash adjustment, Lovejoy?"

"No," I said. "One for one."

"No deal."

"Well, then," I hesitated. "I'm not really in the jade field any more, but . . ."

"No?" He actually laughed. "Then what are we arguing about?"

We began dealing. It's done by mental palpation, not actual

122

utterances. You talk all around the subject, how difficult things are, what clients want nowadays, how troublesome barkers are. We ended with Beck accepting the glass bowl and the jug, plus the painting, in exchange for the jade coin. He took the instrument as well and paid a few notes to make up the difference.

He carried his trophies into the waiting taxi.

"Here, Lovejoy," he said from the window as the car turned in the lane.

"Yes?"

"I don't see why I should pay the driver."

I paid up with ill grace and watched the taxi dwindle uphill toward the chapel. He'd paid anyway. He'd be jubilant, until he found out.

Still, I'd not been untruthful. "That Palmer looks wrong to me, somehow," I'd said. And I'd told him of the instrument, "I'm not sure what you'd call it."

I stood in the garden tying my jade to a string to wear around my neck under my shirt. Contact with living human skin really does restore life and glow to jade. Never leave jade untouched if you can help it. It's the only antique of which this can be said. Jade is the exception which proves my no-touch rule. Even the funeral pieces from ancient China recover their life and luster by being fondled. Love, folks, as I said, is making it. Jade tells you that.

I totted up. I'd sell the mote spoon to Helen. That would pay Janie back and, with what I'd got extra from Beck just now, give me the fare to the Isle of Man. As for the rest, I'd just swapped one set of forgeries for another. Right?

Yes, right. But there was a balance, the money Beck had just given for the jade at Gimbert's. He had successfully bid for it against fierce opposition. I was proud of him.

I'd promised to ring Janie and say what I'd decided to do, but then I thought it over. It'd be better just me against Edward Rink.

I went in to pack.

Early morning and I was on the train to Liverpool.

16

The train's the easy bit.

I like the sea. It's natural, somehow never fraudulent. From the ferry wharf I gazed down the Mersey out to the bay.

If Bexon was right, Suetonius had probably sailed from Chester. The more I thought about it the more it fitted. The Roman Second Legion had been stationed in Chester when Boadicea vented her spleen. That's known nearly for absolute certain. The wily Roman had left his harbor base firmly held in strength, the most orthodox of all military moves. He'd hardly have needed it protected this way if he'd sailed from Wales because the powerful Queen Cartimandua, as nasty a piece of work as ever trod land, was too busy ravishing successions of stalwart standard-bearers in Manchester to notice if the political weather outside changed much from day to day.

The ferry was two-thirds full with passengers. I must have expected a few logs loosely lashed together because I gaped at this huge ocean-going boat. It had a funnel and round windows and everything. Cars were streaming aboard, even lorries.

You can get a meal or snacks and there's a bar. The general impression's a bit grubby but a few hours is not forever. I like wandering about on ships. It being latish September, holiday-makers weren't too plentiful, only a few clusters of die-hards catching the cheaper rates of early autumn. We were a mixed bunch. There were the usual tribes of businessmen discussing

124

screws and valves over pale ales, hysterical crises over lost infants finally miraculously found again where they'd been left in the first place, and couples snogging uninterruptedly on the side decks. They're my favorite. If Janie had been with me she'd have said not to look at them, then looked herself when we'd gone past. Women do that.

Liverpool began to slide away. I looked everywhere on the ferry for my watcher. Twice I went around the lower decks, strolling among the cars and pretending boredom. No sign. He wasn't on board. I must admit I was rather put out. You eventually feel quite proud, being shadowed. After all, not everybody gets trailed, if that's the right word. Maybe he'd been laid off. I already knew that good old Edward was of an economical turn of mind. That meant Rink would be flying first class, of course. I just hoped he'd have sense enough to leave Nichole behind. If there was going to be any rough stuff I didn't want her involved.

Sea gulls cawed and squawked for nothing. They went and sat floating in our wake a lot. Somebody once told me they can actually drink sea water. They have this gland for handling the sodium or something. We had over a hundred following us out of the Mersey estuary into the open sea. You'd think they'd get tired because they've only got to find their way home again.

Ships are noisy, not just the people but the engines, the sea, the floor, the walls as well. Even the funnels make a racket. Somebody always seems to be ringing bells in the downstairs rooms. I went up into the air though the wind was cutting. A sheepdog came and sat near me by the railings.

"Are you lost?" I asked it. It smiled like they do and edged closer to lean on my leg. We looked at the sea rushing past below us. "If you're lost, mate, there's not much hope for the rest of us, is there?"

It said nothing back. I bent down and peered. It had nodded off, probably fed up. I knew how it felt. Me without antiques, the dog without a single sheep. I pulled it away from the railings for safety and hauled it next to me on a wooden seat. When you lift dogs up they seem to have so many ribs.

"Some bloody watchdog you are," I told it. "What if we were sheep?"

I nodded off too. It's the sea air.

*

Ships docking unsettle me. I'm not scared but they seem to head toward the walls so fast. Then the whole thing shakes for all it's worth and stops. Some men threw ropes from our front end. Two chaps on land pulled them around a big iron peg set in the stone road, a queer business. Some others did the same at the back end. We all marched up a flat ladder thing and crocodiled up the stone steps to the town of Douglas, Isle of Man.

"Do you all live on that thing?" I asked the uniformed chap who was seeing us off. He seemed surprised.

"Where else?" he said.

It's a rum world.

I humped my case along a glass cloister affair and crossed over to the taxis. I spent a few minutes describing Bexon's abode, carefully using the same descriptive terms in his diary. One taxi driver nodded finally and took my case.

"Only one place that can be," he announced. "Groundle Glen." I was pleased. Bexon had used that name, though somewhat ambiguously.

The main Douglas beach is rimmed by a wide promenade and a curved road. Houses, shops and hotels gathered parallel for a dense mile or so. Then the hillside begins, suddenly rising to high green fells.

"What's a railway line on the main road for?" I asked him as the north road started to lift out of Douglas town. It had been on my mind.

"For that." He was laughing.

A tiny train, engine and all, was chugging uphill on our left, beside us on the road. One carriage carried the sign *Groundle Glen.*

Ask a silly question.

*

About a mile out the road ran above a small bay cleft in the rock. A cluster of newly built bungalows shone in the late sun. Ships hung about on the sea.

"This is it."

126

We turned right down a sharp incline toward the sea. There were maybe thirty or forty dwellings ribbed on the hillside, mainly grays and browns. New flower beds surmounted bank walls by the winding road.

"Do they have an office?"

"It's only one of the bungalows. A lassie sees to you, Betty Springer."

The taxi driver carried my suitcase to my door. I was becoming edgy with all this courtesy. He praised the view and I tried to do the same but all you could see was the green hillside and woods on the opposite side of the valley and the blue sea rustling the shingle. A stream in its autumn spate ran below. There was a bridge leading to the trees.

"Don't you like the view?" my driver asked happily as I paid him off. I strained to see the town we'd left down by the harbor but couldn't. It was hidden by the projecting hillside. Bloody countryside everywhere again.

"Lovely," I said.

The girl came to see I got the gas working all right as I explored the bungalow.

"The end bungalow's a shop too," she told me. "Papers and groceries. Nothing out of the ordinary, but useful."

"Great."

"Are you a friend of the other gentleman?" she asked merrily, putting on the kettle. She showed me how to drop the ironing board, clearly a born optimist.

"Er, who?"

"From East Anglia too," she said. "Mr. Throop. Just arrived this very minute."

"What a coincidence," I observed uneasily. My private eye?

"I put him next door. You'll have a lot to talk about."

"How do I get a car, love?"

"Hire." She fetched out some tea bags. "I'll do it if you tell me what kind. Have some tea first. I know what the ferry's like."

"And I need a good map."

"In the living-room bookcase. Please don't lose any if you can help it. What are you?" She faced me frankly.

"Eh?" I countered cunningly.

"Well, are you a walker, or an archeologist after the Viking burials, or a tape-recorder man who wants me to speak Manx, or what? Sugar and milk?"

"I'm . . ." I had a brainwave and said, "I'm an engineer. Like my old friend Bexon who used to come here."

"You know him? How nice!" She poured for us both while I rejoiced inwardly at my opportunism. "Such a lovely old man. He'd been to Douglas on his honeymoon years ago. How is he?"

She'd obviously taken to the old chap. I said he was fine and invented bits of news about him.

"He was so proud!" she exclaimed. "He'd helped to build a lot of things on Man. Of course, that was years ago. Are you here to mend the railway? It seems so noisy lately."

We chatted, me all excited and trying to look casual and tired. Betty finally departed, promising to get a car. We settled for first thing in the morning.

So I'd hit the exact place Bexon had stayed. Now, then. Businesslike, I went to suss out the scenery.

The bay window overlooked the valley. Over a row of roofs the light was beginning to fade. Something was rankling, slightly odd. If Bexon was an ailing man, whyever stay at Groundle Glen? Betty Springer had told me the little train stopped near the crossroads up on the main road, maybe four hundred yards away. And an old man walking slowly up to the tiny roadside station could get wet through if it rained. So he was here for a purpose.

The bungalows were too recently built to be of any romantic significance to the old man. There seemed to be only one reason left. I peered down toward the river.

Tallyho?

I went out to buy some eggs, cheese and bread. They had some lovely Auckland butter which I felt like. I bought a miserable pound of margarine instead because the quacks are forever on at you these days. They had no pasties or cream sponges. I found I'd accidentally bought a cabbage when I got home. What the hell do people do with cabbage? I suppose you fry it some way. I opened the windows and looked about for some ducks but saw none. But do ducks like cabbage? I gave up and put it in a drawer.

128

I fried myself an omelet. That, a ton of bread and marge, a pint of tea and I was fit enough to switch on the news to see who we were at war with. Outside hillside creatures stalked and cackled. The sea shushed. The sun sank. Lights came on in the bungalows here and there. A ship's green lamp showed a mile or two off shore.

It seemed a fearful long way to town. When you're in countryside it always does.

*

I got the fright of my life that evening.

It was about midnight. The lights were on in the next bungalow. It was the man who'd followed me. I knew that. Throop. My lights were off. The telly was doing its stuff but I'd turned the sound down.

This figure moved in silhouette. My kitchen door was glass, so he was easily visible. Probably thought I was out. I got the poker and crept to the little passageway. The stupid man was fumbling noisily with the latch. Some sleuth.

I hid in the loo doorway, trembling. My mouth was dry. In he blundered. His glasses gleamed in the part light as I leapt and grabbed him.

"Right, Throop, you bastard!" He was too astonished to struggle. I clicked on the light.

"Greetings, Lovejoy!" It was Algernon, pleased we'd met up.

"You stupid . . ." I let him go. "You frightened me to death."

"Did you not realize?" He went all modest. "I'm being your— undercover agent!"

"Brew up," I told him, trying to keep the quaver out of my voice and trying to hide the poker. I felt like braining him.

"Certainly!" He breezed into the kitchen, falling over a stool. "How perfectly marvellous that someone so perspicacious failed to penetrate my subterfuge!" he nattered, chuckling. He pulled a kitchen drawer out all the way. The crash of the cutlery as it spread over the tiled floor made me jump a mile. Unabashed, he wagged a finger playfully while he grabbed the kettle. "You should have realized, Lovejoy! Algernon sort of goes with Throop!"

"What else?" I put my head in my hands. A spray of water

wet me through, just Algernon trying to fill the kettle.

It was rapidly becoming a bad dream. Here I was trying to slip about quietly, a difficult, risky business with that sinister nut Rink on my tail. I'd thought I was doing reasonably well. Now, thanks to Algernon, following me would be like shadowing a carnival. I had to get clear.

"And I have another surprise for you!" he crowed, plugging the flex in with a blue flash.

"Please, Algernon." I couldn't take any more. My heart was still thumping.

"No, Lovejoy!" he cried roguishly, spilling tea around his feet and skillfully nudging a cup into the sink as he turned. I heard it break on the stainless steel. "I won't tell you! It's a *surprise!*"

Somehow he'd managed to pour hot water into the teapot though it was touch and go and a lot of luck went into it. To save breakages I got the cups. He broke the fridge door looking for the milk which I'd got prominently displayed on the table anyway. He prattled on about his journey, hugging himself with glee about the mysterious surprise he'd lined up for me. I had a headache.

"Push off, Algernon," I said.

"Very well, Lovejoy!" he cried. "Your tea's all ready! See you in tomorrow's fair dawning! And when you wake . . ." He went all red and bashful and tripped head over heels down the passage. The door crashed. I could have sworn something splintered. I listened, wincing. No tinkle of glass, thank God. Another crash. He'd made it home, the next bungalow. I took a sip of tea and spat it out. He'd forgotten the bloody tea bags.

I sighed and looked for a bottle of beer. A secret with Algernon's like a salvo. I'd have to get some sleep. Algernon's secret would be on the night boat. Always assuming her car wasn't too long to fit on the deck.

*

Somebody was in the kitchen again. Light tottered through curtains, still drawn. I vaguely remembered making love when it was dark. I forget to wind watches so there's no point in having one, and those new digital efforts are always trying to prove

130

themselves. I could tell it was about after seven o'clock. I went to the bedroom window and peered out. Sure enough, the Lagonda by the shop.

I climbed back into bed, sitting up. In she came, lovely and floury from waking.

"Morning, Lovejoy, darling."

"I'm supposed to be here alone," I said bitterly. She set the tray right and got back in with cold feet.

"You can't possibly manage without me, Lovejoy."

"It'll be like a Bedouin caravan with you lot. How did you know I was here?"

"Algernon," she said brightly. "I persuaded him your welfare depends on me."

"Anybody else?" I demanded. "Jimmo? The Batemans? Jill?"

"Just me." She dished breakfast out, smiling roguishly.

"You're going back. First boat."

"No, Lovejoy," she gave back calmly. "You've got to pay up."

"Er," I said uneasily. She must mean the sale. "Well," I said slowly, working it out as I went. "I had a lot of expenses. I made about twenty per cent. Fifty-fifty?" I keep meaning to get one of those electronic calculators.

She was shaking her head. It was a pity we could see ourselves in the mirror of the dressing table opposite. She watched me in the pale light. I looked away casually.

"A day. Remember?" Hard as nails, women are.

"Oh." Of course. I owed her a day. I thought hard. Maybe it wouldn't be too bad. I had a good dozen antique dealers' addresses on the Isle. Some were supposed to be pretty fair. "Well, Janie love—"

"Before you say it, Lovejoy," she told me. "No. No antiques. No dealers. No playing Bexon's silly game. One complete day. And I say what we do."

I groaned.

"My hands are hurting," I said bravely. "They're agony—"

"And you can stop that," she interrupted. "It won't work."

"Look, love—"

"We're shopping, Lovejoy." She ticked them off on fingers. "And you're going to cook me a lovely supper. Then you're going to sit with me in the evening, come for a walk and then seduce me in bed. Here. Beneath these very sheets."

"What if we pass an antique shop?" I yelped, aghast. She'd gone demented.

"You will walk bravely past. With me." She smiled, angelic.

I nodded, broken. Ever noticed how bossy women really are, deep down?

"When?"

"Whenever I say." She smiled, boss. "I'll let you know."

Day dawned grimly and relentlessly.

17

I picked up courage while we dressed. "Is this your day?"
Janie thought for a couple of centuries. "No, thank you."
I cheered up at that.

"I have a car coming. Nine o'clock."

"I've cancelled it," she said innocently. "We don't want Lovejoy getting lost, do we?"

Of course we didn't, I assured her.

"Come on, then," I said. "Get your knickers on and we'll look
around."

"Cheek."

We walked down to the shore. The river runs into a curved
stony beach, only about a hundred yards across. The stones are
a lovely blue-gray color. Steep jagged rocks rise suddenly to
form rather dour headlands. In the distance toward Douglas we
could see the gaggle of chalets forming a holiday camp. I'd seen
the sign for it during the drive along the cliff road.

"How noisy." It was a racket, stones clacking and shuffling
and the sea hissing between.

We gazed inland. The shale-floored inlet only ran about two
hundred yards back from the water before it narrowed into a
dark mountainous cleft filled by forest. A wooden bridge
spanned the river there, presumably for us visitors to stroll
across and up the steep hillside. Well, whatever turns you on, I

thought. Then it occurred to me: what if it was Bexon's favorite walk? After all, he had to have some reason for coming this far out of town. Bushes and gorse everywhere. It would be a climb more than a stroll.

We walked over and explored the hillside. The footpath divided about a hundred feet from the bridge, one branch running inland along the glen floor to follow the river. The other climbed precipitously on planked steps around the headland. Janie chose left, so we followed that.

"Look. Palm trees."

I was going to scoff, but they were. The valley bulged soon into a level, densely wooded swamp for about a quarter of a mile as far as I could tell. Somebody years ago had built tall little islands among the marsh, creating lagoons complete with palms. Here and there we could find pieces of rotten trellis among the dense foliage. Once we came upon a large ruined hut by the water. There were at least three decorative wooden bridges.

"Betty Springer said they used to have dances along here."

I wasn't interested. No engineering works, and I wanted evidence. The valley narrowed again a little way on. The trees crowded closer and the undergrowth closed in on our riverside path. The water ran faster as the ground began to rise. I didn't see any point going on. Ahead, an enormous viaduct crossed the valley. The beck coursed swiftly beneath, gurgling noisily. It looked deep and fast. We headed back past the lagoons and took the ascending fork from the bridge, talking about Bexon. The path was only wide enough for one at a time. I told her over my shoulder how I'd got the taxi driver to find the place.

"Are you sure this is where he stayed?"

"Betty remembered him."

Janie really found it first, a brick kiln set in the hillside. Overgrown, like the rest, but reassuring.

"Look how flat the path is here." She pointed out the iron rails set in the ground. The path ran on the contour line seaward from the kiln.

"That's odd. It looks dead level." The flat path was wider now than any other in the hills.

"For hauling bricks?" she suggested.

"Maybe."

It was a little railway. We traced it inland. It ended in a hill-side glade. There we found a ruined station, wooden, collapsed into the forest down the steep slope. We walked back, almost hurrying now. A railway means an engineer. Maybe Bexon had worked on it, probably a scenic run through the woods to view the sea from the headland or something. Of course, I thought. There'd be a junction further inland with the road. And on the road there was still a working steam railway. Hence Bexon's choice of Groundle Glen. It's where his railway ran.

I became excited. We followed the rails seaward. Some parts were quite overlaid by small landfalls but at least you could see where the tracks ran from the shape of the incised hillside. We had difficulty getting past where sections had slid down into the valley but managed it by climbing upward around the gap— using gorse bushes to cling to. We eventually emerged around the cliff's shoulder in full view of the sea. Still the tracks ran on, high around the headland. A tiny brick hut lay in ruins at one point near the track. Curiously, a fractured water tap still ran a trickle of its own down the cliff face. Over the years it had cre-ated its own little watercourse.

The railway finished abruptly at a precipitous inlet, narrow and frighteningly sheer.

"Dear God."

At the bottom the sea had been dammed by a sort of stone barrier set with iron palings, now rusted. It was lapped heavily by the sea. I didn't like the look of it at all. Nor did Janie. I'm not a nervy sort but it was all a bit too Gothic.

"It's creepy," she said, shuddering.

"Why dam it off?" I asked her. "Look across."

There seemed to be a sort of metal cage set in the rock face. It was easily big enough to contain a man. Anyone in it could scan the entire inlet. But why would anyone climb into it? A wave larger than before rushed in and lashed over the rusty barrier. If Bexon had anything to do with building that he really was round the bend. There seemed no sun down there, though the day was bright elsewhere. Some places are best avoided. This was one.

"Come on."

We hurried home, scrambling hurriedly along the railway track until we met the path. From there we took our time.

"It was *ugly*, Lovejoy," Janie said.

She invited Betty Springer over for coffee, a cunning move. We described our walk. I just happened to have the map out, quite casual.

"Your friend used to go over there," she said brightly. "Every day, practically. He used to get so tired. Always rested on the bridge."

"Bexon?"

"Yes. He spent a lot of time walking along the glen."

"Is it an old railway?"

"Yes. For people to see the seals."

"Seals?" I put my cup down. "Seals?"

"You didn't get that far, I suppose." She traced our map with her finger. "Follow the tracks and you come to where they kept the sea lions. You watched them being fed by their keeper. He threw them fish, things like that, but that was years ago. It's a sort of inlet."

Both Janie and I were relieved. We avoided each other's eyes. We'd thought of all sorts.

"Did, er . . . Bexon say anything about it?" I asked, trying to smile in case the answer was not too happy.

"Oh, yes. He kept on about it all the time. He helped to build it years ago," she said.

He would. Not a happy answer at all. If that's where he spent his time, was it where he'd remember something best?

"Why the hell didn't he just stick to railways?" I asked Janie when Betty had gone. "That seal pen's like something in a Dracula picture."

"He mentioned other places."

"So he did!" I said, brightening. "So he did."

"Good morrow, friends!" It was Algernon, wearing a deer-stalker and tweeds. "All ready to go searching?"

"Let's go."

18

We went to buy large-scale maps. I can't do without them in a new place, partly because I always have the addresses of antique shops and collectors about my person.

While Janie went to the grocer's I pulled Algernon aside on the pavement.

"When I tip the wink," I said urgently, "make some excuse to stop the car."

"Why?"

"Because we'll be near an antique shop," I explained. He still looked puzzled.

"Lovejoy. Why is it always antiques?"

I recoiled, almost knocking an old lady down. There he stood in the cake-shop doorway, your actual neophyte antique dealer. Typical. At that moment I really gave Algernon up.

"Never mind, Algernon," I said, completely broken. "It's just something that comes from breathing."

"All ready?" Janie was back. We'd parked the car dead opposite Refuge Tower, now partly sinking its little island into the encroaching tide. "Incidentally," she warned, smiling prettily at us both, "no sudden mysterious excuses to make stops near *unexpected* antique shops. Okay, chaps?"

"What do you take me for?" I said innocently.

I avoided Algernon's accusing gaze as we got in. Janie was

rolling in the aisles so much at her really hilarious witticism she could hardly start the engine.

"What a lovely smile the lady has," I said coldly. "Are they your own teeth?" I only made her giggle worse. That's women for you.

"We're embarking to visualize entrancing spectacles of natural miracles!" Algernon cut in merrily, his idea of light chitchat. Cheerfulness from Algernon's enough to make people suicidal.

*

I'd the copy of Bexon's diary with me. We listed all the named sites, putting them in the same order Bexon had.

"It's less distance," said He-of-the-Blurred-Vision, "and more economical on petrol to proceed circumferentially around Castletown, with—"

"Hold it." I was suddenly suspicious. "You seem to know a lot about these place names."

"So does everybody else, Lovejoy," he said with maddening arrogance.

"Except me," I pointed out. We were gliding upward to the south of Douglas town.

"Motorbikes," he explained. "The races."

I'd heard of the TT races. Naturally, Algernon would know. I'd never seen him without a racing magazine. He started to tell me about engine classifications but I said to shut up.

"We'll do it Bexon's way," I replied huffily. I saw Janie hiding a smile and explained, "It's more logical."

"Yes, darling," she said, the way they do.

"Right, then." We drove on in stony silence.

The Isle's a lovely place. The coolth gets into you quickly. You unwind and amble rather than sprint. Even the Lagonda began coasting, giving the feeling of a thoroughbred cantering on its home field.

We drove that day what seemed a million miles. After each place that Bexon had mentioned I took a vote. I had the veto, because of my detector bell, though Janie complained about being tired after only four hours or so.

138

We drove to the House of Keys at Castletown and from there hit the road to Cronk Ny Merriu's ancient fortwork. Algernon saw some sort of stupid swimming bird there, which led to a blazing row because I expected him to keep his attention riveted on my quest, not bloody ducks. He got all hurt, and Janie linked his arm till I cooled down. The trouble is she thinks he's sweet.

We bowled into Port St. Mary after that, then Port Erin for fish and chips. Another tick, about one o'clock. They wanted to rest but I said not likely. We walked from the folk museum up Mull Hill to the six-chambered stone circle. I loved it, but time drove us off. Janie thought it all rather dull. Algernon saw another duck, so he was all right. The Calf of Man, a little island, couldn't be reached, so we turned back to the main road after Janie had flasks filled at the little café. We climbed the mountainside north of Port Erin to the Stacks, where the five primitive hut-circles were just being themselves. Another tick, and varoom again.

Beckwith's Mines were rather gruesome, like any mine with shale heaps and great shafts running into the earth between two brooding mountains. I was relieved when Bexon's lyrical comments led to nothing. After all, a mine is nothing but a very, very deep hole. It was nearly as bad as that seal pen.

"I don't dig mines," I quipped merrily, snickering, but Janie only raised her eyes and Algernon asked what did I mean. No wonder I always feel lumbered.

The last thing of all was the great peak of South Barrule. We left the car and climbed, walking with difficulty among the dry crackly heather tufts. I was glad when Algernon found something. We stopped. I almost collapsed, puffing. He fell on his knees.

"It's *Melampyrum montanum!*" he breathed reverently, pointing. "What astonishing luck! The rare cow-wheat! Glacial transfer, from Iceland with the Ice Age! How positively stupendous! Oh, Lovejoy! Janie, look!,'

He seems so bloody delighted at the oddest things. I staggered closer and looked. He'd cupped his palms around some grass.

"Isn't it breathtaking?" he crooned.

"It's lovely, Algernon," Janie said. "Isn't it beautiful, Lovejoy?" She was glaring at me. Her eyes said, Just you dare, Lovejoy, just you dare.

"It's great," I said defiantly. I would have praised it anyway, because I'm really quite fond of grass. "Really great, Algernon."

"Nowhere else except this very hillside!" he cried. "What a staggering thought!"

I gazed about. There were miles of the bloody stuff as far as the eye could see. And I knew for a fact that the rest of Britain was covered knee-deep.

"Well, great," I said again. "Take it home," I suggested, trying to add to the jollity. I should have kept my mouth shut. Algernon recoiled in horror.

"What about propagation, Lovejoy?" he exclaimed. "That would be quite wrong!"

So we left the grass alone because of its sex life. Silly me.

And after all that, nothing. We rested at the top for a few minutes but I was worried about the daylight.

"You said we'd do it all in two hours," Janie complained.

"I lied," I said back. "*Avanti.*"

The rest of the search was enlivened by Algernon describing the spore capsules of the *Pellia epiphylla,* while I went over the Viking burials and tumuli we'd seen. Nothing. Still, I trusted my feelings about Bexon. He'd got on to something. Put me within spitting distance and I'd sense it. I knew I would.

I came to with us heading north on the metalled road and Algernon explaining the difference between a bogbean and a twayblade, whatever they were. I'd have given anything for a pastie. Not to eat, just to shut his cake-hole.

    *

That day seemed months long. My mind was reeling with views of yachting basins, harbors, promontories, inlets, small towns huddled around wharves, castles, Celtic burial mounds, neolithic monuments and encampments, tiny museums (musea? I never know the proper declension) and stylish period houses. We finished Bexon's list baffled and bushed. I was knackered. Only Algernon the Inexhaustible chattered on. Janie thinks he's marvellous. She likes talkers. Whenever he seemed to slow up she'd actually ask a question and start him off again in spite of frantic eyebrow signals from me. I swear she likes riling people sometimes. He seemed to know everything about everything except antiques. He even tried telling me there were different kinds of sheep.

"Never mind, Lovejoy," she said, all dimples, toward the end of the day. "We might have had to travel in your hired Mini."

I tried not to laugh but women get through to you and I found myself grinning. Just shows how tired we were.

"Let's pull in," I suggested.

"A mile further on, please, Janie," Algernon asked. "There's a pull-in there." Surprised, we all agreed. It wasn't far from Douglas anyhow, and we'd reached the end of the list, so what did it matter?

I saw why he'd suggested this when we arrived. Even though it was quite late people were milling about. A café stood back from the road on the exposed hillside. A mile further along the hill a television transmitter's mast poked up, its red light shining to warn aircraft. A large stand for spectators had been built on a macadam apron beside the road. Motorbikes littered the ground.

"It's one of the TT checkpoints," Algernon beamed with delight. "Look! An Alan Clews fourstroke! Good heavens!"

I went in and got some pasties. Three teas in cardboard. When I emerged Janie was back in the car trying to keep warm. A wind was getting up. Algernon was admiring a cluster of bikes. Some were in pieces. Enthusiasts in overalls and bulbous with bike gear compared spanners. What a life.

"Isn't it a positively stimulating scenario, Lovejoy?" Algernon said, really moved. It looked a hell of a mess.

"Eat," I said, thrusting a pastie into his mouth.

God help the Almighty when we all come bowling up to heaven, each of us with a different definition of Paradise. I wish Him luck. And if everything there's lovely and new I for one won't go.

"Thank you, Lovejoy," he said. "Come and see this Villiers engine."

141

"No." I'd rather his rotten grass than his rotten engines.
I gave the grub out.

"Oh, Lovejoy," Janie complained. "I hate this soya stuff."

"I asked for it." If you save only one cow a year it's a lot. Indeed it's everything, if you're the cow concerned.

"We've finished, love," Janie said pausing. "He didn't mention any more places."

"Don't nag."

She gave me a searching look and then tried to cheer me up with questions about Suetonius and Co. I was too dejected to respond. The trouble is I tend to get a bit riled when I'm down.

Wearily I leaned on the car. In an hour it would be dusk. The motorbike fiends were undeterred by mere changes in the environment. Algernon was joining a group busy stirring a heap of metal tubes on wheels with spanners. One oil-daubed bloke even seemed to recognize him and shook Algernon's hand.

"I'm so sorry, darling." Janie put her hand on mine. "I wish I could help."

I shook her off and looked about, simmering.

"Lovejoy," she said warningly, but I was beyond talk. I'd nothing against the bike fiends, but I had to sort somebody out for light relief. I was suddenly breathing fast and angry, all my hopes in ruins. Yet I *knew* we were close. One small clue . . .

"Lovejoy. *Please.*"

Over in one corner was a little group clustered about a couple of soapboxers. One was a bird from the Militant Feminist League. I ignored her, though I'm on their side. I really do hope the suffragettes get the vote. I needed somebody worth a dust-up. And there he was, the inevitable rabble-rouser, I saw with satisfaction. You get at least one where there's a crowd. He had a soapbox near the café steps. My blood warmed and I moved casually toward him.

"*Lovejoy.*"

I heard Janie come after me. I honestly wasn't spoiling for a fight, but these political nerks do as well as any. You can't go wrong because they're all stupid.

"You're all capitalist dupes and lackeys," he was yelling, an unshaven political gospeller. He got a few catcalls and jeers back from the bike fiends but kept going, a game lad. "Your bike

142

races are personalized general crimes!"

I drifted past Algernon. He was asking the others about plugs.

"Joe Faulkner'll have a spare," a voice replied from underneath a bike.

"Lives up near Big Izzie," another explained. "Anybody'll direct you to her." The lads laughed along with Algernon. Some local joke.

Algernon tried to interest me in the bike's pipes but I strolled on to hear the politician. I'd give him five minutes' skillful heckling, then I'd cripple the bastard.

"It's the day of the Common Man!" he shouted. Nobody was listening. "The day of equality is dawning! Share all! Possess all! Equality, the word of the age!" One of those.

He was really preaching against antiques. I hate jargoneers, as Florence Nightingale called folk like this twerp. It's today's trick, urge everybody else to be mediocre, too. People everywhere talk too much about the Common Man, what a really terrific bloke he is and how anybody different's either a secret anarchist or fascist at heart. It's all balls. Let's not forget that the Average Man's really pretty average.

"Nobody's ever equal," I pointed out loudly. "It's a biological and social impossibility. Inequality's right," I said pleasantly. "Equality's ridiculous."

I honestly believe this. I've been striving all my life in the glorious cause of inequality.

What can you say to stupid bums like this, that shut the Sèvres porcelain factory so we could all have none?

"Clever dick," he sneered. "Piss off. Go and piss Izzie round."

A few of the bike fiends who overheard laughed at this crack from beneath their tangles. Probably that local joke. I began to move toward him happily, then stopped. Izzie? Anybody'll direct you to her, they'd told Algernon as I'd passed him. To her. Female. Izzie. Isabel? Isabella? Piss Izzie round—like a wheel? It reminded me of something.

Janie came hurrying over. She'd collected Algernon.

"We really ought to be going," she was saying as they arrived. I was watching them approach. "We're all too tired to think. I can cook us a hot meal. It's been such a tiring day. We need a rest." She looked at me, worried. "Lovejoy?"

"Is anything the matter, Lovejoy?" Algernon asked.

"You're so pale," I heard Janie say. "Has he said something to offend you?" She spun angrily on the startled orator and snapped, "You keep your stupid opinions to yourself, you silly old buffoon!"

"No, Janie. Please." My mouth was dry. "I'm so sorry," I explained gently to the speaker. "It's my first visit here. Where is Big Izzie, please, Comrade?"

"I knew you were one of us deep down, Comrade," he said, smug with pride. "It always shows through the capitalist-imperialist veneer. Comrade Marxist's definition of class illustrates—"

"He never defined class," I said. "He promised to in that footnote to his first German edition, now very valuable, but never got around to it. Big Izzie, Comrade. We've a, er, political meeting near there."

"Laxey," he said. "We ought to get together, Comrade, to discuss class fundamentalism—"

"It's a date," I said. "Laxey, you said?"

"Long live the revolution!" he called after us.

"Er, sure, sure!"

I rushed them to the Lagonda and had Janie hurtling us toward the road to cheers and waves of the surrounding multitudes of the bike people. She was screaming for instructions at the fork but I didn't know where Laxey was. We scrambled for maps, then two cars came by and we had to wait till they passed.

"Laxey?" Algernon said at this point. "Go left."

"Sound your horn!" I cried in anguish, but anyone who beeps a horn in Britain is either on fire or psychotic. Janie's upbringing held firm. We moved sedately out onto the Laxey road.

"Who'll be there?" Algernon asked pleasantly.

"How the hell should I know who lives in Laxey?" I said, baffled.

"He means the meeting," Janie began to explain. "There isn't really any meeting, Algernon, you see. It was a—a ruse."

"There's an enormous waterwheel at Laxey," Algernon said brightly as Janie gave the car its head.

"Then why didn't you say so?" I hissed. If I'd not been in the front I'd have thrown him out.

"Is it what we've been looking for all this time? Its picture's on the coins."

I fumbled in my pocket. It bloody well was, the imprint of a great waterwheel. One day I'll do for Algernon.

"It's even got a name," he continued cheerfully. "Lady Isabella. They say that when it was first made—"

"Algernon!" from Janie, tight-lipped. Algernon had known all along, the stupid sod.

I closed my eyes. Sometimes things just get too much.

*

The wheel's beautiful. You know, the Victorians really had it. If a thing is worth doing at all, they obviously thought, then it's worth doing well. On the side of the supporting structure was a plaque: "Lady Isabella." There she was, gigantic and colorful, pivoted with such exquisite balance that a narrow run of water aqueducted downhill was sufficient to power her around at some speed. She was breathtaking.

She was set in the hillside valley near a stone bridge. A deep crevasse sliced into the hill, exposing a ruined mineshaft. Old discolored mine buildings eroded slowly, block by block, higher up. An enormous, massive beam projected skyward from the ruins, probably one arm of a pump of some sort for the underground workings.

"How colossal!" Janie said it. Colossal was the word.

There were steps up from the path to its main axle. Algernon rushed up to see the giant waterwheel swinging its immense height skyward.

"Imagine the size of the bike engine you'd need to—"

"Algernon," I interrupted. "Don't. No more."

Janie was watching me. Just then she tapped me firmly on the shoulder.

"Well, everybody!" she cut in brightly. "Home time."

"*What?*" I rounded on her.

"Home time, I said." Janie put her hand on my arm like a constable.

"We've only just got here!"

"And now we're going. You owe me a day, Lovejoy."

145

"But you said it wasn't today," I yelped. "And we've found her! My main clue!"

"No," Janie said. "It *wasn't* today, Lovejoy. But today's over. Look."

I came to. The day had faded. Our car was the only one left in the car park beside the river down below. The little toffee shops had closed. In the distance lights showed where the seaside promenade of Laxey lay. Lights were coming on in the cottage windows. An old woollen mill blotted out the foreground. Mill owners of years ago had laid out the valley like a stone pleasure garden, now somewhat sunken and ill-kept. It was swiftly quietening into dusk.

"But, Janie, for God's sake—"

"It's dangerous, Lovejoy," she said in that voice. "Derelict mines, ruined mine buildings, horrid great pumps underground and a wheel this size. If you weren't so deranged by being near whatever the poor old man left, you'd realize how exhausted and frightened you really are." She took my arm. "Home."

I tried appealing to Algernon but he backed down. Friends.

"I claim my day, starting from this instant," Janie said. "Twenty-four hours."

Women make me mad. They're like the soap in your bath. You know it'd be good value if only you could find out what it's up to and where it is.

Algernon was nodding. "True, Lovejoy. You're bushed."

"There, then!" cheerfully from Janie. "We're all agreed."

I was defeated. I looked up at the Lady Isabella.

"Check the time, Algernon," I said coldly.

"Twenty past eight."

"Twenty-four hours, then." I waited for orders. "Well?"

"Home chaps." She fluttered her eyelashes and waggled seductively down the steps ahead of me. "You'll thank me later, B'wana, when we're all cosy."

Algernon joined in.

"Never mind, Lovejoy," he said brightly. "There's always another day."

I didn't speak to either of them on the way home. People who know what's best for you give me a real pain.

19

"What if Edward Rink's come over after us?" I asked. I'd got fed up sulking.

"Don't argue. You need the rest. You're a wreck."

"And what if—?"

"Rest." Janie was painting her toenails reddish. "A normal day's what you need, Lovejoy." I was reading. "Look how much good it'll do us. You get too involved in antiques."

"I could have it by now." I nearly dropped my drink just thinking of it.

"Rink's man's stupid. You said he couldn't follow a brass band. No sugar for me, please."

I brewed up and carried her cup over. She was on the couch by the window. We could see Algernon stalking some innocent sparrow across the field. I sat watching her doing her nails. They blow on their fingers but not their toes. I suppose toes are too far down even with knees bent. She has a little enamelled case full of small tools for things like this. French women used to have small cased sets of hooks and needles for unpicking gold-fringed decorations and embroidery. It's called drizzling, or parfilage. Women to the last, they'd collect the gold thread in a bag and sell it back to the goldsmith-embroider, who'd then make a lovely gold-fringed item, such as a bookcover, with an appropriate expression of devotion woven in. Then he'd sell it to a suitor,

who'd give it to his lady love, who'd take it to the theater and un-
pick the gold thread and put it in a bag and sell it back.
. . . Women may be very funny creatures but I never said they
were daft. The unpicking sets are now valuable antiques and
not uncommon. Gold fringe embroidery of the eighteenth century is, as you've guessed, very rarely found. Incidentally, this
pernicious fashion was ended at a stroke and we actually know
who stopped it. The writer Madame de Genlis condemned the
habit in her novel *Adèle et Théodore* in 1782 and it vanished
like snow off a duck. That saved a few rare pieces, now naturally worth a fortune. Light a candle for her, as I do occasionally.

"We go shopping." Janie spoke emphatically.

"Er, great." I tried to sound straining at the leash. "Me too?"

"You especially."

"Well, great."

"Then we have a lovely quiet meal together." She fanned her
toes with her hand. "Algernon can eat alone. Elsewhere."

"Where do you cut your toenails?"

"In the bath."

Funny that. We know the most intimate secrets about everyone throughout history except for toenail cutting. There's no
really accepted etiquette. So you do it in the bath. Well, well.

"Couldn't we go past Isabella?"

"No."

I gave in, but there'd be no half measures. I decided I'd make
the meal, a really posh one complete with garnish. I stood
watching Algernon in the distance, thinking, what's garnish? It
sounds some sort of mushroom.

*

In the town we had a splendid time shopping, I mean, really
breathtaking.

It's great. You trudge along a row of shops, then trudge back.
Then you trudge between two or three shops which all have the
same stuff. Then you trudge about searching for a fourth, also
identical. Then you trudge back and forth among all four. Then
you find a fifth. You keep it up for hours. As I say, it's really
trudging great. We got Janie some shoes. It only took a couple of
months or so.

148

I cut loose and bought the stuff for our meal, following the advice of a booklet which told me about the teasing of my taste buds by *tournedos bordelaise*. It sounded really gruesome but I persevered. It seemed to be some sort of meat with gravy. I met Janie under my mound of vegetables. She fell about laughing, but I replied coldly that I was working to a plan. We went shopping for a few more years before returning to the bungalow where I crippled myself cooking for the rest of the day. I learned my least favorite occupation. It's cooking. Janie sent Algernon out to eat.

By evening the kitchen looked like Iwo Jima. We started our meal elegantly, holding hands now and again over the tablecloth. Well, so far, so good. But it'd be touch and go making love later on.

I was knackered.

*

That evening Algernon came in and said he'd have used a little more thyme and possibly a shade less garlic. Janie pulled me off before I could reach the cleaver. Then he made me feel quite fond of him by eating everything left over.

20

I got rid of Janie and Algernon among the cottages where people park their cars. It's forbidden to drive right up to Lady Isabella. I was quivering with excitement.

"You'll miss me up there, Lovejoy." Janie sat watching me go.

"No, I won't," I called back. In an hour or so I'd own a wealth of genuine Roman golds. Mind you, I thought uneasily, I'd told myself that a couple of mornings ago and finished up bushed and poor as ever.

"Good luck," from Algernon. He was geared for lunar orbit. A pal was lending him a motorbike.

I climbed the steep road above the river. Where it turned right and humped upward toward Lady Isabella I glanced down. Janie waved, small now on the flat stones by the water. I plodded on between the cottages. At the café I resisted the temptation to look. She ought to have gone by now because I'd said to, but I knew exactly what she was doing. She was noting the time. If I wasn't down in a couple of hours she'd come after me with the Army. They never do what you say. I heard the crackle of Algernon's bike maniacs arriving.

The wheel was even more huge in early daylight than it had been in the dusk. One could stand on the paving and look upward. From there the paddles were hurled swiftly toward the sky, dripping water where they thinned abruptly, then vanished, replaced by other swift, soaring slats. I made myself giddy watching. Curious how a simple motion can be exhilarating and even beautiful. The clack-clack sound so close became almost numbing after a few minutes. I shook the feeling away and cast around.

The wheel was fed by a narrow stone aqueduct which ran from a hillside cleft to the left. One of the unpleasant facts was that the derelict mine shafts lay that way. The good bit was that the huge beam pump wasn't working, thank God. It looked gruesome enough as it was, still and silent. As I'd thought at Beckwith's mines, a mine is a terrible intrusion into the earth, almost an offence against living rock. I could understand a mountain getting mad, like when the volcano erupts in those old Maria Montez jungle adventure films. Anybody'd feel annoyed if a stranger suddenly barged in to root in the larder to see what was worth pinching.

A few early visitors arrived while I was gaping at the wheel. Judging from their knowing reactions I must have been the last person on earth to hear about Lady Isabella's existence. It was very annoying. They milled about exclaiming at the beautiful machine. Yet . . . no bell, no ding-dong.

I walked around as far as I could go. Then back. A group of visitors climbed the steps down which Janie had wriggled so seductively to entice me home the evening before last. We saw the tremendous humming axle, the radiating struts seeming so gigantic they were like so many fairground complexes, stolen and cast into some skeletal giant. I touched and listened, touched and listened. Nothing. A rather matronly lady was giving me the eye. A month before I'd have had to, because I like older women, but being this close to my find gave me a greed-based willpower. There was no time to waste. I drifted away, leaving them gaping at the axle.

The road became a mere track up the incline, very stony and almost precipitous in parts. To the right the cleft below became practically a ravine, littered with fallen masonry and chimneyed mine vents. A narrow goyt spun water out of the rock and let it fall abruptly. God knows what cold deep subterranean chasm it squeezed up from. About halfway up the hillside the crashing noise of the water ended. I noticed the sound of Lady Isabella had faded.

I stopped to rest on the wall of a shallow stone cistern, wondering what Janie was doing. The great wheel turned silently down in the valley between me and the sea. Lovely.

It was about ten o'clock. The pale sun was catching the wheel's colors and flicking them about the mountainside. The main beams started out a silvery gold. By the time they flashed onto the dark browns and greens all about me they were a brilliant tangerine, a Thai enamel silver box's color. They make these boxes now, real silver but cheap. There are only about six modern designs knocking about so far, basically an opaque white or a translucent tangerine. Dishonest people are said to use deep-heat physiotherapy lamps and two hours' cooking at the back end of a good quality vacuum cleaner without its filter bag, to mimic the appearance of antique enamel. It works, but only if you look from a mile off. Look with a microscope. Uneven crazed surface equals modern, faked. Even surface, with the occasional large deep "bubbled" area, may be the real thing. Give me first offer.

A motorcycle skittered into view, way down below on the Laxey road, the rider anonymous in his bulbous helmet. Funny old place to be riding, I thought. I rose and began the climb again. Maybe he was training for a scramble race cross-country. Whatever it was, he was booming up the track behind me like the clappers.

I was only a hundred yards from the most ghoulish of the mine shafts when the bastard nearly ran me down. Now, it could have been an accident. I admit that. The track was only about four feet wide there. Like a fool, I had my eye on the mine ruins, not bothering to glance behind at the approaching rider. Maybe my apprehension was focused uneasily on the workings. Whatever distracted me, I was hellish slow, only managing to chuck myself to one side and not completely escaping. The maniac's handlebar slammed into my hip, spinning me like a top. There I was, clinging dazed to the stony bank while the dust shower settled. He didn't even stop.

My shirt and trousers were both torn. You could see the bruise swelling and blueing before your very eyes. Ugly. I was shaking so much it took me three goes to lift a stone and put it on the lump. I wetted it from a hillside ooze and sat there trembling, trying to press the damp cold stone to my side to stop the swelling. The trouble is, once a person's inside motorbike gear he becomes unrecognizable. He hadn't seemed heavily built. Quite slight, encased in leather crammed with insignia and no number plates that I could recall.

Three or four times I fancied I could hear a distant crackle but wasn't sure of the direcion. My hip was murder when I pulled myself together and resumed walking. I carried the stone to chuck at the swine if he came back. It's funny what goes through your mind after a bit of a scare. Algernon's thin. He's also a bike fiend. The rider was too small for Beck. It was too crude a method for my friend Edward Rink, and anyway he'd only to knock me off *after* I'd found the stuff for him, not before. I wondered if the rider could have been a woman. Not Janie, surely. Kate? The question was, did he/she really attempt to do for me? Or was it just a stray stupid rider showing off?

I was opposite the mine shaft. I stopped to listen. Nothing again. Water welled from the rock and ran along the aqueduct in a steady flow. I was out of sight of the wheel now. No houses, no people. Only derelict buildings, the ungainly beam engine projecting its huge arm, the trickling water and the stone track.

From where I stood the cleft was only forty yards wide. What had they mined in those days? It looked grim on a pleasant sunny day like this, with holidaymakers trekking up to the café and then down to the sea for dinner. On a rainy winter's day it must have seemed to the miners like a freezing hell.

Old Bexon must have been tough if he'd come all this way. Could an elderly man, gradually sickening in his final illness, climb down from the track, across the cleft and into the mine? I limped back and forth for some time. There seemed no way across. Maybe it would be wise to follow the path to the crest. The miners had had to get over there somehow in the old days, and I could make a quick check to see if that bloody rider was lurking over the hill or not. I was starting to hurt and had to rest a minute. I threw the stone away. Seven long seconds to hit the bottom of the shaft with a faint splash. A hell of a fall, even for a stone.

Bleak places have this effect on me. I get restless and start working out how far's civilization. Not that countryside isn't great on a postcard but it needs watching. I only want Wuthering Heights not to spread about too much. A hundred yards further on I found the causeway. A series of small arches had supported it, but now only their stubs stuck upward from the little valley's floor. Some wise man had dismantled it. I'd have danced from relief if I hadn't just been injured. If there was no way across for me there'd been no way across for old Bexon. It couldn't be done. And lugging a lead coffin over there would need a helicopter. I was saved. No dark, deep hidey-holes for jubilant Lovejoy. Home again, still empty-handed. I turned back, relieved but disappointed.

I went over the possibilities on the way down. A list of named spots—nothing at any of them. The most likely spot was here, near Lady Isabella. But I'd got no vibes near the wheel herself. And in any case she was well maintained, cleaned and painted. Obviously had plenty of vigilant engineers about and was, from what I'd seen, a popular tourist spectacle. The wheel seemed far too public. Yet some place near Lady Isabella was obviously the place a man like Bexon would remember best. *Wasn't it?*

Janie was sitting on a big flat rock near the car park chucking stones into the water. She'd taken her sandals off and her feet were wet. Her frock was up over her knees.

"Hussy," I called down from the bank. I was still delighted about the mines. "I can see all up your legs."

"Cripple," she said angrily. "I heard you limping. I told you to be careful." She was mad again. "Did you fall?"

"Now, don't start, Janie lovie," I said. Why do women keep getting so mad when they should be all worried? I honestly don't get it.

"Don't you lovie me, Lovejoy."

"Where's Algernon?" She looked up curiously. I'd tried to sound casual.

"Off on a bike. He told you."

"Of course," I said, easy still. "So he did."

She pulled herself up the river bank and stood inspecting me. "Stop looking at me like that," I complained. "I feel for sale."

"What happened up there, Lovejoy?"

"Nothing."

"I'd better have a look at it." She pulled my torn trouser away from my side. "Dear God." A family passing to their car exclaimed and tutted sympathetically. I moved away from Janie's fingers.

"Don't show my bum to everybody."

"We'd better call at a chemist's for some ointment."

Inside the car was hot. Janie put the air conditioner on.

"Where to, B'wana?" she asked. I put my head on her.

"Love," I said, "I just don't know."

*

That night I couldn't sleep. When that happens I always think, well, so what? Okay, so I'll be a bit tired next day. All the better rest you get the night after. There's no need to be as distressed as some people get. But Janie was tossing and turning, too. Maybe it was the lingering effects of my grub.

Fitful patches came, blurred and then left me starkly conscious. I've heard that people mostly worry about work during the dark hours. With me it's faces. They came gliding into my mind like characters from a Kabuki play. Some just wouldn't go. Helen, for instance. Maybe I'd imagined her down at the shops yesterday, result of a subconscious longing, perhaps. We'd been very close but only briefly. The stress of competing for the same antiques had torn—well, snipped—us apart. What was she doing here? The antique shops, possibly. But "possibly" also means possibly not. Then Kate the Wicked Sister, with her single-minded message not to help Nichole. Not surprising, really, because womankind occasionally has been known to be slightly tinged with the sin of jealousy, so it's said. But how could I possibly help Nichole, when she insisted on going about with that murdering pillock Rink, instead of a lovely hunk like me? Algernon's too thick to be anybody's ally, I told myself, isn't he? *Isn't he?* I got up at one point and padded in my pyjamas to peer through the back door glass toward his bungalow. No lights. Well, three in the morning. But was he in there? Or maybe he was stealing back that very second to Big Izzie, having seen something I hadn't. I cancelled that possibility and slipped back into bed. The idea of Algernon stealing anywhere's an absurdity. Even when he brews up it's like a fife band. Janie stirred. I let my legs get warm before closing in on her.

Then there was Rink the Fink. No good wondering why a rich man like him wanted to bother with a possible find of possible valuables. Greed knows no rhyme or reason. I've actually seen a real, live millionaire cover his face and weep uncontrollably in a famous Bond Street auction for carelessly missing a Penny Black—admittedly these stamps aren't all that common, but you can find them if you look carefully. I got up again.

There was no light from the hillside. I sat in an armchair after pulling the curtains back. Who was actually doing the watching? Or was there nobody there at all? I had this feeling again. Supposing Rink had two watchers, twelve-hour shifts. Possible, but how the hell would they contact Rink if I made a sudden dash anywhere? Some form of field transmitter? I gazed out into the darkness. Maybe the watcher and I were looking directly at each other, unseeing. Unless he had one of those night telescopes. Was he smoking out there? You can see a match at five thousand yards. That's what the sergeant used to say, on his belly in the mud, refusing to let the lads smoke two whole leech-ridden days before the ambush. I moved the armchair uneasily. There's something really rather nasty about being looked at when you don't suspect. It's a sick feeling.

Janie was trustworthy, though. I pondered a long time about Janie. Wealthy, lovely, and humorous. Exactly what the doctor ordered. You have to trust the woman you sleep with, don't you? I mean, if you can't trust the woman you sleep with, whom can you trust? I mean to say.

It was so dark outside. I could just see the skyline. There were some stars. The forecast said it might rain before dawn.

Yet Janie never trusts me. She keeps saying so. Still, that was easily accounted for—women aren't very trusting people by nature. They are a very unusual sex, when you think of it. I don't think they'll ever be the same as us, reasonable and even-tempered. What lingered unpleasantly in my mind about Janie was her husband. We'd never spoken about him, not properly. And she'd never mentioned him since that night except once to say, when I'd asked, "Yes, that was my husband you heard. He only stayed a minute." She goes back to him, though, most of the time. Whenever he returns from abroad she zooms home, the dutiful wife. And what was happening between them now was anybody's guess. I didn't even know where she was supposed to be this very moment, with a sick auntie at Broadstairs or what. I suspected she'd made him believe she was legitimately absent on some benevolent enterprise. But husbands get philanderers followed. They're known for it.

Lastly, Beck. Well, maybe the fact that I'd whittled him for the odd doubloon had filtered down through his cerebral cortex by now and he was doing his avenger thing. Most unlikely, really. Beck was a sort of positive Algernon, a mad bull compared to a gormless spaniel. He'd have crashed in here the minute the ferry docked: Lovejoy, you swine, did you whittle me?

Something moved out in the night. A patch of darkness suddenly became cohesive and shifted slightly. I knew it had been six feet or so to the right a minute before. Dark's solid where living things are. My hands groped about the armchair. Great. Caught without even a stone or a poker, in pyjamas. The black grew larger. Dear God, I thought, sweating, it's coming right up to the window. The window darkened to one side. I was so tightened up I couldn't even screech for Janie. A faint gleam on spectacles drenched me in a sweat of relief.

It was sodding Algernon, the stupid bastard.

I blundered to the window and scrabbled for the catch muttering I'd kill him, frightening me to death like that.

"Lovejoy." A whisper.

"What?" I croaked back, third go.

"He's out there. Do you want my night glasses?" He was whispering where the windows met. This was it. Dandy's killer had finally come.

I forced myself to push the window gently open. Cold air streamed blessedly in.

"Where?" Never mind *where*, Lovejoy, for God's sake, ask who. "Who?"

"The badger." He sounded surprised.

"Eh?"

"Shhh, Lovejoy!" he hissed in anguish. "You'll distract him!"

A bloody badger.

He got a three-minute whispered torrent of invective. Once one person whispers everybody does it and nobody can stop. Ever noticed that? Contagious, like yawning.

I deliberately slammed the window and went back to bed. Once I'd got warm again and my terror had lessened a bit I began thinking. In spite of myself Algernon's stalking impressed me. How come that he was normally so clumsy? Maybe daylight did things to his coordination. I couldn't tell Janie about the incident. She'd only laugh and tell me what I should have done.

That's the trouble with hangers-on, I thought bitterly as I nodded off. I'm on a three-seat tandem. We all want to honk the horn but nobody wants to pedal.

*

It must have been in one of those semiconscious states that my logic did its stuff. Tandems. My dopey dawn mind saw a tandem ridden by Kate and Nichole. Then it took them away and put the diaries there. Then it put the two sketches there.

I awoke at six stark with cold fear. *All Bexon's pointers were in twos,* everything from the Roman babes on the gold coins, Romulus and Remus suckling on the she-wolf. Everything. Except for one lonely, horrid, decayed nightmare place, one terrible exception. So obvious. Suddenly so clear.

Dear Jesus. The inlet.

It had to be the seal pen.

Creeping out of bed, I rose and tiptoed about.

21

I should have spotted it earlier.

His hiding place'd had to be near Groundle Glen. Had to. Otherwise, why stay here? His diary said "... it's convenient." There was only the old railway line and the seal pen. I'd walked the length of the tracks several times and seen nothing. There was one place I'd never inspected close to, though. And that was the seal pen. Courage, Lovejoy.

I was out at first light. No signs of life from Algernon's bungalow. Janie slept on. I hurried down toward the bridge and climbed up the path to the diminutive railway. There wasn't another soul awake among the bungalows. I was clear away. I trotted on.

In the dawn light the seal pen scared me more than ever before. The cleft seemed to run a thousand miles down to where the sea struggled over the stone barrier. Most of the palings on the narrow wall had rusted to jagged points with fallen pieces lying obliquely to trail nastily into the sea. I wondered if any seal had ever managed to escape. Surely they must have wanted to. It was like a bad stage-set nicked from Wagner's Teutonic worst.

A concrete platform with a wonky railing was the only sign of civilization where the railway ended. I was frightened. The ledge was pretty dangerous even on a calm, sunny day. What it looked like on a stormy night didn't bear thinking of. I edged my way cautiously onto the platform, feeling like a figurehead on a ship. I'd never seen so much sky around.

The heather and the grass had created a bulge where the tiny rails ended. There were probably buffers under there, overgrown. A circular rim set in the concrete level looked oddly familiar, reminding me: a gun emplacement, probably antiaircraft. They'd built the platform wider and stuck an ack-ack weapon on top, for the war. Which miserable gunner battery had snapped up this particular posting? Poor sods. They'd have had to struggle back along the railway in the dark even to fill a kettle from the leaky tap at the ruined brick hut. Well, at least they could have used the little train for hauling shells. To me they were heroes as brave as any fighter pilot. I looked down again. The nightmare cleft had deepened a few miles since my previous glance. Did it go up and down with the sea? Was its water connected underneath all that stone and rusted iron? There was a noise behind me. A sheep rolled its mandible at me over the wire fence.

"Bloody fool," I said. "Go away. I'm scared enough as it is."

It didn't shift. I've never been able to tell people off.

The cage on the other side of the inlet was set on a lower level than the platform where I stood. A dice-tumbler, I suddenly realized. That's what it reminded me of. Another Bexon joke? It had been constructed on a slight prominence, giving it for all the world the appearance of an iron pulpit projecting out over the seal pen. There was no way in except through the top, where the metal staves were curved toward their common center. You could get in but you'd have a terrible time getting out.

I could see across into it. Some rubble. Double iron doors in the cage, one shut with a grille at eye level, the other ajar. Maybe it was a further wartime addition, which suggested there was another way in from the landward side, probably with steps cut down into a tunnel. That's how they made entrances to dugouts in the trenches. Soldiers don't change much.

At one time there had been a catwalk across. I could hardly bear to look. Not that I'm scared of heights, but there's a limit. It had deteriorated over the years to a crumbling bar of weathered concrete spanning the sixty or so feet across the gorge. Most of the iron struts and handrail were gone. The entire thing was rust-stained, which gave it a horrid toothiness I found distinctly unnerving. The inlet must be like one great mouth if you looked from the sea.

The noise again behind me. The sheep hadn't gone.

"Can you see anywhere else it could be?" I asked. It said nothing. You get no help.

Getting around to the other side would be bad enough, let alone climbing down to the iron pulpit.

"Shift," I said. The sheep stepped away from the fence.

Intrepid ramblers obviously came this way, along the overgrown railway track. It was only about as wide as a small path anyway. The one safe way around the inlet was to climb up the steep hillside into the sheepfold, walk over and descend from the hillside onto the cliff top again. I did it, clinging to the barbed wire for all I was worth and not looking down.

I was quite calm and pleased until I glanced back at the old gun platform. Had I just stood on that? And looked *down*?

The platform was as thin as a match, a little white scar marking a rising mass of jagged rocks. Below, sea waves, pretty docile until they swept casually around the headland, rose into white claws and scrabbled viciously at the volcanic rock. It made my feet tingle. And Bexon's gang had somehow built a seal pen in this savage place. More annoying still, he'd come back to see it years later.

I found the entrance to the tunnel cut through to the pulpit, and the steps I predicted. The hillside had slid gently into it, simply folding the passageway in the rock. There was no way through. Worse, clearing it would take a million years. Two million, on my own.

My rope had some iron things on that the man in the ship chandler's yesterday had said would hold on to anything. A likely tale. I latched them mistrustfully to the tunnel upright, a beautiful thick post reinforced with a metal bar for a hinge. It was set solidly in concrete top and bottom, a lovely great piece. "Stay there," I told it, "and don't budge. Please." For extras I made a couple of knots (well, eight, actually) around the opposite post in case. I'd previously examined every inch of rope a few hundred times, peering for flaws and hidden gaps. Now I did it again, rubbing it through my hands and feeling for any old razor blades or chewing insects I'd overlooked. It seemed all right but suddenly very thin. Had I put on weight? Thoughtlessly, I'd had a glass of milk, which now made me mad. I'd have been just as strong without, at least for a few hours, and I was bound to be heavier. How stupid to eat like a horse. My school science came rushing frantically to my aid. A pint of water weighs a pound and a quarter. But it had only taken one bloody lightweight straw to break that biblical camel clean in two, and everybody knows how tough camels are. I tried spitting out to make myself lighter but my mouth was dry. I drew deep breaths to get rid of some water vapor from my soggy fluid-crammed lungs but only made myself so giddy I had to stop. I tried peeing, politely turning toward the vacant sea away from the sheep, but couldn't wring out a drop. I'd dried up. Maybe I was so dehydrated with fright I'd faint and fall, turning over and over, toward the . . .

"Now, Lovejoy," I said. "Be reasonable."

How reasonable is it, I heard myself begin to answer back sharply, to dangle . . . ? I moved quickly to the edge and found the double bush of heather I'd picked out as a marker. With luck I'd be directly over the iron pulpit. I was chary of my recovering hands, though, and made a million false starts. The strength was there but so were the twinges. Hell, I lectured myself sternly. They'd once shown an infant three days old happily dangling by its own hands from a clothesline. I'd seen it on telly. And if a sprog could do it. . . . I slithered untidily down, clinging to the rope and babbling incoherently with fear. Not that I was really frightened, not too much. It's daft to let yourself get too scared. I shrieked with terror when the rock surface momentarily vanished underneath me. I hung in space staring upward. The crest was only a few feet away. I seemed to have been going down for hours.

You mustn't look down. That's what they say. Then how the hell can you see where you're going? I had to. I forced my gaze along to my elbow, then made it leap the gap to the wall of rock. It travelled down on its own from there. Down. Down. My belly seemed to leave me and vanish, falling. My legs prickled. The sea was green, so deep and green. Mad white rims poked and swirled. The concrete gums and iron teeth seemed actually to be moving, gnawing erratically at the sea's body and running white blood back into the ocean. But the most fearsome thing of all was the iron pulpit. It was only twenty or so feet from where I swung but its very oddness and its nearness set me moaning. The hole at the top was smaller than I'd imagined. The rest of the cage was disproportionately larger. Funny, that.

A lunatic wind whistled around the rocks from seaward, making me dangle a few degrees from the vertical. I should have looked to see how much rope I'd got. I tried to but couldn't. How long I hung there I don't know. What finally started me moving down again was a sudden spasm of fear. My hands were sweating. They might slip and set me falling, turning over and over, toward the . . . I inched down, thinking suddenly, Dear God does sweat dissolve nylon? I might land down there in the iron pulpit, find the stuff and finish up trapped with half a ton of melted rope.

My moaning was interrupted by a scream. It was me. I looked down. The top curled iron staves of the cage had touched my foot. I found I'd curled up on the rope, my body balled as tight as possible in a spasm of reflex clutching. Stupid sod. I forced my reluctant leg out and crooked my foot around one bar. It seemed staunch enough. I pulled myself nearer. There was enough rope to reach. I could trail the end into the cage with me. Even if it came undone from inside the cage sooner or later it would flail within reach under this huthery wind. Hanging on for dear life to the line with my left hand I grabbed at the pulpit with my right hand and held on to the lovely strong iron. It's extraordinary how you want to keep curling up. I tried to bring the rope and my left hand nearer but only succeeded in clinging like a sloth to the cage's ironwork. Sweat poured down my face yet I was grinning with delight at all this success. Even the rope was miraculously behaving, having somehow looped itself over my shoulder. I needn't look any more. The worst part was straightening both legs and dropping into the cage. I found I'd kept hold of the line, probably not trusting the concrete floor of the cage. It may sound daft but at least it's careful.

I examined the interior, avoiding the ghastly spectacle of the seal pen barriers directly below and trying not to hear the sea sounds sucking and gasping. Everything looked fairly solid. The metal was rusted but mostly intact and hard. I couldn't bend it or shift any of the palings. Cast iron, the old Bessemer process. The concrete only reinforced living rock, I saw, so the chances of the base giving way under my weight were virtually nil. It was exactly five feet wide. That was where my luck ended. The stone, concrete and ironware hadn't been displaced or touched since the whole thing was made. Bad news, Lovejoy.

Which left the recess. Presumably the tunnel ran to emerge somewhere back there. I examined the iron wartime doors first. Both were rusted in place. That's modern metal for you. Rubble had fallen from the walls and made it difficult for me to squeeze in. I could hear water trickling and dripping in the dank blackness. Would there be bats? Peat. It stank of peat. Did peat give off fumes like those that gassed you in coal mines? I had a pencil torch. But, I worried, are those little bulbs electrically insulated so they can't touch off an itchy explosive gas? Why the hell is all this never written on the bloody things? They always miss essential instructions off everything you buy nowadays. I was so angry I took the risk, cursing and swearing at manufacturers. No bang. The light showed me a brick-lined space about four feet wide. The start of the tunnel. The sea down below gave a louder shuffle which made my heart lurch. A few soldierly graffiti indicated the last time anyone had stood there. Dust covered the floor. The tunnel's infall began a couple of paces from the iron doors.

It had probably been deserted after the war. Weather, perhaps mostly rain and seeping water, had weakened the tunnel walls. Bexon could never have been here. I edged back into the daylight, still pressing the surface with my foot as I went. No sun seemed to strike into the sea-washed cleft. You'd think they would have built the seal pen to catch a lot of sun, if only for yesteryear's holidaying spectators. Lord, what a day out it must have been. I'd have paid not to come. I wasn't unduly perturbed when I didn't see the rope exactly where I'd left it. Ropes hanging free swing about, especially in winds. Actually I couldn't remember knotting it carefully on an iron upright but I'd worked it out. I'd soon catch it as it flicked past.

I looked about from the cage. The sea had risen somewhat but could never reach the pulpit. There was no sign of a tidal mark this high. Safe as houses. The trouble was I couldn't see the rope at all, flicking about or otherwise.

Oddly it didn't concern me much at first. It was probably caught up somewhere, maybe on a clump of heather or on a small scag of rock-face. It had to get blown free sooner or later, hadn't it. Hadn't it?

"Lovejoy." Rink was waving from across the crevasse.

I didn't answer immediately. All I could think of was rope.

"Yoo-hoo," he called. Not a smile. That's the sort of character you get in antiques nowadays. No soul. He'd won hands down and not even the glimmer of a grin. He was alone.

"What?" It took me two goes to croak it out. It suddenly seemed a long way over there. And back up the cliff. And down. It was a hell of a long way to everywhere. Bleeding hell.

"Find it?"

"No."

"Then good luck, Lovejoy. That's all I can say. Good luck."

"What do you mean?"

"You'll need it."

He sat on the platform. The swine had a hamper. He took out some sandwiches and a flask. He seemed prepared for a long siege. It all seemed so exasperatingly strange at that moment. There was Rink, in his smart suit, noshing an elegant picnic breakfast. And there's me stuck in an iron pulpit like a caged fly in a gruesome grotto. His very appearance of normality was grotesque.

"I watched you arrive from the hotel window," he told me affably. "Quite good service. Sherry's brought to you chilled here. Odd."

I'd guessed right. That pathetic hack sleuth must have passed word I'd left. Rink had flown here hours before me.

"I can climb out, Rink," I managed to squeak after swallowing a few times.

"No, Lovejoy." He was maddeningly calm. "No. Look at the cliff."

I'd already done that. I didn't need to do it again.

"Where's the rope?" I called lamely.

"Quite safe." He poured a hot drink for himself. "Don't try."

In a panic I jumped and caught on the incomplete roof of the pulpit. Better to try climbing out now while I was fresh than after being trapped a whole day—a week? Something cracked sharply. The rocks near my left side spattered with ugly suddenness. My cheek ran warm. I dropped back. Rink was smiling now. He had a double-barrelled shotgun.

"I won't run out of cartridges, Lovejoy," he assured me.

"Bastard."

"I'm only anxious to preserve your life."

"Why?" I asked. Maybe Algernon had heard the gun and would come searching. But there were a lot of hunters after pigeons knocking about. I'd seen them about the middle of the island. One more shot wouldn't be noticed. Anyway I couldn't encourage Rink to keep on using that thing. It was a modern hammerless cartridge ejector, I saw with scorn, when you can still find brilliantly engraved antique hammerlocks of the early percussion period. They're even cheaper than good modern guns, the burke. He could have used a luscious Forsyth scent-bottle fulminate percussion weapon, damascus-barrelled and silver engraved. What a slob. Honestly, some people, I thought. It really shows a typical low mentality.

"You'd better start, Lovejoy."

"Start what?"

"Guessing." He waved a sandwich at me. "I can wait. Every guess you give will be painstakingly investigated, Lovejoy. If the box is where you say it is I'll return and drop your rope over."

"And if not?"

"Oh, you'll be allowed as many guesses as you like. Take your time."

"How do I know you'll come back?"

He smiled again, then. What worried me was that he wasn't sincere. It should have tipped me off but I suppose I was too scared right then. Oh, I know he'd been painstaking and finding me had cost him a quid or two. And he'd risked a hell of a lot, killing Dandy Jack like he did. But that spark was missing. I should have known. Every single genuine collector I've known is always on heat. Mention the Sutton Hoo gold-and-garnet Suffolk cape clasps to a collector and his eyes glaze. He pants like a bulldog on bait. He quivers. There's music in his ears and stars glitter in his bloodshot eyes. Your actual collector's a hot-blooded animal. Not Rink. I'll bet he did pure mathematics at school. I ought to have realized. Unfortunately I wasn't in a thinking mood.

"I'll shout for help," I threatened. Some threat.

"I dare you. Ever seen lead shot ricochet?" He was right. One blast directly into my pulpit would mash me like a spud in a grinder.

"Don't talk with you mouth full," I said. He took no notice, just sat noshing and gazing at the scenery. "What if I don't guess at all?" I shouted over.

"I can wait. Day after day, Lovejoy. You'll die there."

"And the knowledge dies with me, Rink."

"Don't be illogical, Lovejoy. If you know," he said reasonably, "it's a consequence of your visit to where you are now. Or else, it stems from what's in the copy of Bexon's little books, which doubtless you carry on your person. As soon as you're dead I shall come down and have access to both sources of information."

"I don't have them anymore." Lying on principle.

"They're not at your bungalow," he called. "So you must have."

"My bloke'll come searching soon." Get that, actually threatening a maniac with Algernon. The cavalry.

"I've taken care of that." He sounded as if he had, too.

"Er, you have?"

"I left them a note saying you'd gone home. Told them both to follow you as soon as possible, urgently."

"I'll do a deal," I called. He said nothing. "Rink?"

"You're in no position to do any dealing, Lovejoy."

"All right," I said at last. "I know where the stuff is."

"Tell me."

"No. I want . . . a guarantee." That's a laugh, I thought, an antique dealer *asking* for a guarantee. A record. It'd make a good headline. Antique Dealer Demands Guarantee as Typhoon Grips Ocean . . .

"You're inventing, Lovejoy." He was looking intently at me.

"I'm not. I do know. It's true."

And all of a sudden it was.

I yelped aloud as if I'd been kicked, actually screamed and

brought Rink to his feet. I knew *exactly* where Bexon had put the gold. I could take anybody there. Now. A place I'd never seen, but the precise spot was there and I knew it almost down to the bloody inch. I could see it in my mind's eye. The wheel. The water. The Roman coffin. Splashing water and the pompous lady of the sketch in her daft one-wheeled carriage. I was smiling, even, then chuckling, then laughing. What a lovely mind the old man must have had. How sad I'd never met him.

"I know!" I was laughing and applauding, actually clapping like a lunatic as if a great orchestra played. I laughed and cheered and jigged, banging my palms and taking bows. I bounced and shook my bars. "The old bastard!" I bawled out ecstatically, laughing and letting the tears run down my face. I practically floated on air with joy. If I'd tried I could have flown up and landed running. "The beautiful old bastard!" I roared louder still with delighted laughter. "The old bugger's had us on all along!" And I was on the selfsame island, the very ground where the Roman Suetonius had landed, pouring his Gemini legion on the Douglas strand. History was wrong. Bexon was right. The clever old sod.

"Where is it? Where?" Rink was on his feet, puce with rage.

"Get stuffed, Rink!" I screamed merrily, capering. "It deserves *me*, not a frigging cold lizard like you, you—"

"I'll—" He was raising the gun in a rage when he seemed to jerk his legs backward. Perhaps he slipped. He gave a rather surprised but muted call, not even a shout, and tumbled forward. The shotgun clattered on the platform. I watched, frozen, as he moved out into the free air above the yawning seal pen and started to turn downward. It was a kind of formal progression. I can see him yet, gravely advancing in a curve, arms out and legs splayed as if to catch a wind. Only the scream told it wasn't as casual as all that. It began an instant before the body dropped tidily onto the iron stakes on the crumbling stone barrier. Rink seemed to move silently once or twice as if wanting to settle the iron more comfortably through his impaled trunk. An incoming wave began its whooshing rush at the inlet's horrible mouth. His limbs jerked once before the sea rushed over him. An arm moved slowly as if reaching into the trapped lagoon of the seal pen. The wave sighed back, stained dark. Oddly, it only

168

became a deeper green from his blood. There was no red. I was staring at him some time. He must have been dead on impact, I guessed. What a terrible, horrendous word that is. Impact. There's nothing left once you've said a word like that, is there? Impact. I was shivering from head to foot. Impact. I was violently sick inside the cage.

The worst of it was the sea kept moving him. It seemed as if he was alive still, trying to rearrange matters so as to make a slight improvement in the circumstances in which his corpse now unfortunately found itself. The start of a demented housekeeping in his new resting-place. I turned away and retched and retched. Lighter now, I thought wryly, maybe an easier climb.

"Lovejoy," a pale, shaky voice called. I could see nobody.

"Who is it?"

"It's Nichole. Are you safe?"

"Is there a rope up there?" A pause. Please don't let her have fainted or anything. "Nichole?"

"Yes." Her voice carried distantly down the cliff. I strained to see her. "It's fastened to the wood."

"Don't pull it off!" I howled in panic. "Don't touch the fastening. Just chuck the free end over. And keep back from the edge." I repeated the instructions time after time in a demented yell until I saw the rope come. I tugged it, swinging on it as a test. "Does it look firm to you?" I shouted.

"Yes." She didn't sound so sure. I swarmed up, holding the free rope between my feet as I'd seen circus climbers do to lessen the strain on my hands. It seemed an age but, knowing me, couldn't have been longer than a couple of millisecs.

I sprawled gasping on the rock at Nichole's feet. Why hadn't I noticed it had started raining? The poor lass was weeping but quite honestly my sympathy for others was a bit used up. I crawled away from the edge and rose shakily. We embraced, Nichole trembling and heartbroken and me quivering from relief and eagerness. It wasn't far to Bexon's hoard.

"I was so afraid," Nichole said. "You were so calm and brave. Edward was like a mad thing. He kept making me help."

"Thanks for the rescue, love," I said. I moved us further inland. Neither of us wanted to see the inlet and its seal pen ever again.

"Is—is Edward . . . ?"

"Let's go straight home." I comforted her as we walked toward the sheep. A group was watching. They looked so absolutely bloody calm. What right had they to be so unconcerned while I'd nearly snuffed it? I was furious and made them scatter with a sudden shout to teach them a lesson, the smug bastards. It was all right for them. They were safe in a field of their own.

"Don't we have to tell the authorities?" Nichole asked. "Poor Edward."

"In a minute," I said. "I'll show you my bungalow first. It's in Groundle Glen. Not far. You can rest there. I've got something to do. I'll only be a few minutes."

Janie and Algernon would be gone, Rink had said.

We got through the wire into the fold. The sheep had assembled on the landward side. I avoided their accusing eyes as we made our way over the humped field and clambered down to the overgrown railway. Well, I thought defensively, they could at least have looked just a little bit anxious on my behalf. People are far too bloody complacent these days. Just let a sheep get into trouble and it expects shepherds, collie dogs, a wholesale search, the lot. Sheep have even got a parable to themselves, selfish swine.

"Look, love," I said. "About poor Edward."

"He was obsessed with these fanciful stories," she sniffed. "He made me—"

"Yes, darling." I explained how we'd better just go. People would assume it was some ghastly hunting accident. Nothing could be done for him now, anyway. She took it really well. I said she was a brave lass.

Neither Nichole nor I looked back at the inlet, nor down into the water. We left the platform with Rink's gun and its open hamper. The sea gulls would handle what was left.

I was still smoldering when we came within sight of the ruined terminus. I pointed out the bungalows across the valley from among the trees.

"See that one with the smoking chimney?" I said.

"Near the blue Lagonda?"

"Eh? Oh, er, yes." Well, well. Janie was supposed to have gone chasing to the ferry. "Anyhow, three roofs to your right.

That's it." I gave her the key. "Wait there for me. I'll be back smartish."

"Edward's car's there too," she sniffed. "We had the bungalow next to the shop place." Cunning old Edward.

No wonder I'd felt watched. Like the fool I am I'd worried myself sick about the view from the window overlooking the fields and the sea. And all the time Rink had been sneering at my back, laughing like a drain. Even now my neck prickled. I vowed I'd never be that daft again.

"I'll not be long." I saw her off where the footpath wound down from the railway. She kissed me. Twice she turned to wave. I watched her go. I didn't move until I saw her slight figure appear on the valley floor below. She walked out upon the wooden bridge and turned to wave again, shading her eyes at me. I waved and stayed put. She stepped on to the metalled road, heading up to the cluster of bungalows.

I ducked behind foliage and raced along the railway track.

You can't blame me, really. The law of treasure trove says firmly that the person finding precious archeological stuff is entitled to the treasure's value. No messing about. So if you find another priceless miraculous dump of "old pewter," as it was called, like that pop singer did at Water Newton—incidentally now the brilliant centerpiece of early Christian silver exhibitions the world over—you claim its market value. The coroner fixes the money for you with independent assessors. Naturally, you can't keep the actual trove itself. That usually gets stuck in the British Museum or somewhere. But you get the market value. Fair's fair. The trouble is that *two* equal finders are made to share equally by the nasty old coroner, who cruelly wouldn't trust Lovejoy to be reasonable. After what I'd been through I deserved at least sixty per cent, I told myself as I hurtled through the undergrowth along the steep hillside. If not seventy. In fact, I was reasoning as I ran breathlessly by the ruined terminus and started down the steep stepped path toward the waterlogged forest floor and the clumps of palm trees, I really deserved it all.

There must have been torrential rain somewhere on the uplands. The river was in hectic spate. Even the lagoon water was swirling. I noticed that several of the small overgrown weed islands were partly submerged. The run was taking it out of me,

171

probably the aftereffects of the climb and Edward Rink. I was astonished to realize blood was running down my face. My own blood. Then I remembered, just before fainting with fright, that he'd taken a shot at me. A rock chip had caught my face. It really had been a hard day.

I slowed to a jog along the narrow river path, then a walk. Finally I reached where the tributary beck trickled beneath its elegant bridge. I had to sit on a wayside stone for breath. Only now it was no trickle. It was a tumbling, spouting cascade, which had dropped an octave from an innocent, lightweight chuckle to a deep, threatening, lusty boom. Spray watered ferns high above and the ornate bridge was quivering with the sustained impact of the falling water. God help fishes. I rested longer than I meant to.

I pushed on. It wouldn't be far. The steep valley narrowed sharply at the next bridge. Despite the full daylight, now the water noise and the steep forested rock sides made the scene claustrophobic.

It was a real hiding place for Druids on the run. Opposite the ruined wooden shelter that Betty Springer had said people used for parties I had to rest again. I panted and gazed at the vegetation. Algernon had said the glen was famous for its celandines, bluebells and wind anemones, but like all flowers they're just basically different sorts of eccentric dandelions. Two days before he'd tried to show me a monstrosity called a bladderwort that ate insects, the maniac. I edged away from some long-stemmed red flowers and pressed on upstream. They looked full of appetite. The brick uprights of the causeway showed among the trees ahead. I crossed at the last bridge to keep to the main path.

The viaduct was gloomier and darker than ever. Janie and I had never gone all the way beneath. Now, the rush of the swollen river caused the path to be flooded by a nasty swark. The three races, parted for the giant columns of the overhead road, emitted as they ran a sustained bellow, which echoed and intensified between the brick pillars. Thoughtful Victorians had cobbled the path but forgotten a handrail. People were made of sterner stuff in those days, probably. I pushed on sideways along the path to the cobbles and stepped into the flooded bit. It was only a few inches deep this high above the river but still rushed with disquieting force against my ankles.

Beyond, the glen couldn't really be called a glen anymore. There was very little space from wall to wall. It was more of a dark crevasse whose walls were encrusted with polished tubers of igneous rock mortared by ferns and lichen. Trees soared upward, practically meeting in a great knitted entombing arch two hundred feet high. The path stayed beside the hoarse river, now demented by the addition of gray-black honed rocks. I plodded on, occasionally having to take hold of a tree branch for my weight where the path was either too overgrown or vanished completely. Algernon had told me they were beech, fir, birch, alder, willow. Their names sound all garden and tea-on-the-terrace, don't they, but down in Groundle Glen they were having a hell of a time of it. They were twisted and scrabbling for toeholds up the soaring valley walls. One had fallen here and there, slamming down into the river or lodging across the boulders. I was struggling breathlessly over a slain skinned trunk and thinking that some lunatics do this for fun and call it rambling, when I saw it, a few yards up ahead. I yelled out for joy, clawing up through the undergrowth toward the wheel.

If everything was twinned in Bexon's trail, what else for Big Izzie but a Little Izzie? And where else but along the very glen where he'd stayed? An old, sick man just can't get far, especially with a digging job to do. I'm stupid, really slow.

The river rose to a natural series of bouldered waterfalls. And that exact point was where, years ago, Bexon had sited his little ornamental waterwheel, a beautiful simple copy of the original Lady Isabella. Her twin. If I'd had any sense I should have guessed: two identical diaries, two sketches, two nieces, but the carriage in the picture he'd chosen to copy had only one wheel. Find the missing thing and you're there. Stupid Lovejoy. I'd stayed in the same glen and never worked it out.

A decorative wooden millhouse stood amid engulfing greenery, maybe thirty feet tall. It was painted a crumbling black and white, typical Tudor in style, to offset the faded yellow of the wheel itself. Trust old Bexon to get the colors right this time. Guessing now where the path probably went, I hauled myself toward the millhouse, breathless with excitement. My chest was suddenly tightly constricted, clamoring and clanging. Warm and getting hotter. I stubbed my foot on a stone. Steps ran—lurched—upward. A rusty old handrail showed in the foliage, curving along the rock wall toward the millhouse. Of course. In those days the people were families on a day out. For safety there would be no way to the actual waterwheel except maybe for a man to work it. I clambered up the steps. The handrail looked pretty precarious so I kept away and tried pushing myself along the rock face among the honeysuckle and brambles. I smelled sweet but was gradually being shredded. The steps curved narrowly up between the incised valley wall and the millhouse planking, very similar to one bend of fairground helter-skelter, with the millhouse representing the tower and the steps the slide. It was about as steep. Twenty steps and I was almost level with the roof.

The path was rimmed by railing from there and ran level but higher, perhaps to climb steadily along the glen to emerge eventually on the main sea road, but I couldn't see beyond a few feet because of the day-dusk of the overhanging rocks and the dense vegetation. The river was three feet below me where it started its torrential dash to the boulders. A wooden lock gate had once diverted the flow from the millwheel's blades. Now the wood was rotten. The river split on a big pile, spraying a race against the wheel in a high bow wave. The wheel showed a gear on its millhouse side, maybe half the full wheel's diameter.

Where else but in the millhouse?

The walls seemed fairly substantial. I tested by pushing the planking carefully. Stable. I guessed the wheel to be about ten feet tall. If that gearing was still in working order the turning force of a millrace in this sort of spate would be colossal. Decorative, but dangerous. I'd have to be careful. There were no windows on this side but a diminutive platform projected over the waterfalls. Entrance therefore from below. I clambered down and peered up at the millhouse.

It's surprising how big things look when you're feeling vulnerable. The millhouse seemed supernaturally tall and thin. From high up I could have sworn the wheel, clapped so firmly to its side and spurting the rushing water aside into an aerial jet to join the rest of the torrent, was no more than ten feet in diameter. From below it had grown. I was standing level with its lowermost blades. Only the merest trickle crept out from beneath, a testimony to the builders' skills. Stray trickles are wasted power, energy just chucked away. Even in decoration craftsmanship tells. I splashed the few yards through the muddied undergrowth. A wooden platform, crumbling, about chest height.

The millhouse's downstream aspect showed four turreted windows, two and two, not large enough to enter. I hauled myself onto the planking making two give away instantly. I tumbled through onto the fetid mud beneath the platform. I was in a hell of a state and cursing worse than usual. But if the platform was fixed and I was the first to plunge through, then nothing could have been hidden beneath, correct? I was grinning like an ape, sweating in the dank air and almost bemused by the percussions of the booming river. This close, the falls were indescribably ugly. I've heard people go over in coracles for fun. They're welcome.

The platform creaked and spat splinters as I crept across it on hands and knees to spread my weight. A hinge, smugly veiled by its grime, was a foot from my face. Part of the wooden wall was crosscut, just as you see in stable half-doors. I found the finger hole after groping, and pulled. Naturally I fell beneath it as it tumbled out, but that's what comes of slow mental processes. Doors open, rotten doors fall outwards. The interior was a revolting mess of bird droppings and feathers. A set of wooden steps and a platform on the riverward side seemed more trustworthy than the outside planks, perhaps because they were protected from weathering. I crept up, jogging cautiously and waiting for the creaks to subside before trying the next step. The wheel was visible through a slit. I pulled at the edges. Rotten pieces came away in my hands. The whole structure was dicey. Only the gears were intact and they were practically perfect.

The wheel was a working model, connected through its gear to an internal cogwheel about four feet across. Every single depression had been packed by grease, lovely thick grease, and the cogs were as clean as the day the gears had been cast. A solid locking lever held the teeth. Carelessly I unslipped the chain peg to see what happened. The wheel gave a great scream as its gears clanked round. I yelped and almost went through the crumbling floor. The outside rushing noise lessened instantly as the water pushed the wheel blades.

I looked out. The great bow wave had gone from the waterfalls. Instead the millrace was busily turning the waterwheel, but nobody could get near the thing to examine it while it was heaving round. The great thing sounded alive, whining and groaning and sighing like that. It unnerved me. I leaned back. More wood came away. I judged the turning cogs exactly right and hauled the lever into place. The distressing human noises stopped and outside the bow wave spurted again. I'd rather have that going all the time than the horrid shrill whines from the wheel. I locked the lever firmly with its peg. It was rigid enough without it, but accidents happen. One kick and the wheel'd be off again, so careful. I'd had enough risks to last the day out.

The bird droppings below showed there'd been no disturbance for years. Every sign in the whole narrow millhouse indicated somnolence with nothing moved or replaced. I glanced upward into the roof beams. You could see the entire recess, even to the odd feather stuck to the ties. Take away roof and walls and floor, and that leaves what? I couldn't reach any of the windows but they too looked as untouched as the rest. There was no real door. I stayed where I was for a minute to work it out.

Yet somebody, a devoted old engineer weary with years and illness, had carried a heavy tin of grease—not to mention a Roman lead coffin—along the glen and restored the simple machinery to pristine state. He'd greased axles, levers, every cog. That alone was a labor of love, because the wheel must have required stopping and starting a few dozen times. It had been a nervy business for me. For him less so, but at least as exhausting. I pulled at the platform. A piece of wood came away near the gear wheel's axle. Nothing hung there. And a Roman casket's no matchbox. It's not the sort of thing you can tuck in a spare corner. No ledges, no shelves. A hollow millhouse. The gears themselves?

I felt in my pockets. A comb, a pencil, a few coins. I scraped at the inner gear with a milled edge. Whatever the metal, it was solid and not gold. That only left the outside. I stuck my head out through the slit. Seen from out there, the whole world seemed full of surging waterfalls. The waterwheel was inches from my face. Despite the wind and spray I could see the mill-race's surface where the wheel blades deflected the torrent. I noticed the water-run for the wheel. How clean the stone slabs were down there. How very, very clean.

Now, why leave the wheel stopped? Engineers say machines are always better used. But it was locked. So the millrace channel obviously needed to be kept dry. Perhaps while somebody went down and removed a slab—one of those clean slabs—below? Or perhaps to show the way? If you risked a climb down the millrace while the wheel was turning you'd be squashed like a strawberry between two stones. Thoughtful old Bexon. I pulled back in, ecstatic. My bell was clanging delightedly. That old chest feeling was still there even when I heard her shout.

"Lovejoy!" She was below, but very close. "Are you in there?"

"Yes. Stay there. I'm coming down."

"I'll come in."

"No need, love. The platform's unsafe."

She came crawling in anyway. I reached the top of the wooden stair.

"Did you find them?" Nichole's eyes were shining unnaturally bright. She looked lovely.

"Why did you bring that bloody gun?" She must have been scared by the gloomy woods.

She was smiling impishly. One good thing, she was as out of breath as me. "I came after you, Lovejoy. To help, in case you got hurt. Did you find them?"

"I've guessed. It's here. The millrace, behind the slabs." I'd been first. The coroner would have to acknowledge that.

"Show me, darling."

She hurried creaking up toward me. I yelped and tiptoed back. The struts couldn't take both our weights.

"For Gawd's *sake!*" I told her to go easy.

"Show me!"

"Not here, darling." I smiled and reached a hand to her. She smiled up at me and pointed the twelve-bore.

"Yes. Here, darling." There was something funny about her smile. Her eyes were brighter still.

"Eh?"

"Show me, Lovejoy." It was her eyes. She wasn't making a polite request. I was being told.

"It isn't up here," I said lamely. "It's down *in* the millrace."

"Where?"

"Have you loaded that?" I asked. Her smile became a little less diseased. A trace of humor showed.

"Certainly."

"Look, Nichole, love." I'd have to treat her gently, if only for the wonky platform's sake. "All this has upset you. Let's get outside. This place isn't safe." I edged toward her.

"I ran over Dandy Jack," she said brightly, all confidence. "So don't think I'm chicken, Lovejoy. I'll pull this."

"That sod Rink." I quite understood. He was one of those sick cold people who impelled more normal people into lunacy. "He forced you to do it. Never mind, love. He's gone. We—you and me—can manage without the others now." I pointed. "It's hidden behind the pale slabs below the waterwheel."

"Is it really there?" She peered timidly out. So help me, I actually steadied her by holding her elbow.

"For certain," I told her, smiling. "Can't you hear the lovely radiance?"

"Why!" she exclaimed delightedly. "So I can!"

She suddenly came back inside, staggering slightly as a board cracked and gave way, straightened up and shot me. What with the water noise, the sudden apocalyptic crack of the gun, the bewildering realization of what had happened and being spun around by the force of the blow in my side, I was disoriented. I heard somebody screaming, not me for once, a high steady insane call. I was on the ground among the bird droppings and bleeding like a pig. I wondered why it didn't hurt. The rotten planking had given under the weight of us both. We'd been tilted different ways, me inside and Nichole out into the millrace. God Almighty, the millrace. My arm was stiff and bloody as well. Most of the shot had missed but I'd collected a hell of a lot of blast. She'd fallen through the rotten boardwalk. My arm was stinging. That smell was powder. Nichole. That was her screaming somewhere.

"Nichole!" I yelled, coming to. She screamed again. "Hang on. I'm coming, love," I shouted, coughing from the acrid fumes of the gun's explosion.

I hauled myself back up the steps. She wasn't there, but a great torn hole let the crazy view in, the still wheel, the hurling water and the tumbling drenched rocks rising abruptly above the falls.

"Please, Lovejoy!" she was screaming. "Darling!"

"Hold on!" I called. "Hold on!" The force of the gun and the rotten platform giving under us had thrust her back against the wall and it had simply fallen away. I spread myself on the platform as quickly as I could and slid toward the gap. She was lodged between the wheel and the stone slabs, head mercifully out of the onrush.

I'd have to risk my arm and shoulder under the wheel. I examined the locking lever, in case. It looked exactly as I'd replaced it. One careless nudge against the peg could edge the cogs into place and the entire bloody waterwheel would turn, sweeping Nichole down and crushing her against the sliprace stone slabs. And I'd go too.

"Please, Lovejoy!" She was moving, becoming frantic now, in worse danger of slipping further under the wheel.

"Hold on!" I screeched. "Hold on!"

"I can't!" she gasped. Water was pushing against her head.

"You must! One second!" I yelled into the roar. "Drop the bloody gun!" She was holding mechanically on to the gun, for God's sake. As if it was any use. I turned aside to see if there was anything for me to hang on to. Not a bloody thing. Nichole must have feared I was going away because she screamed.

"*Lovejoy!*"

"I'm still here, darling." I turned back to reach into the flood for her arm. I couldn't lose her now, not when I'd everything in my grasp. As long as I kept my legs clear of the gears and that huge ominous lever. "Lift yourself," I bawled, getting a mouthful of the water. "*Now.*"

179

"I—I didn't mean to." She was babbling incoherently as our hands met. I pulled. Nichole started to come free of the water. I gasped at the exertion. My side was hurting now, but we were clinging firmer. I began to wriggle slowly back along the wooden platform. "I didn't want to kill your birds, Lovejoy darling," she gasped.

"*What?*" I yelled. Her relieved smiling face was an inch from mine. We were both practically submerged, me dangling upside down, hanging on, and her draped on the wheel in the funnelled mountain water. She still clutched the shotgun. As if I hadn't enough to lift.

"I knew you'd forgive me, darling," she said breathlessly. I still held her in an embrace. "And the bike was a silly joke."

"*You?*" I shrieked.

"And I just *had* to push Edward . . ."

I was still pulling her up but now I stared in horror. She must have seen my eyes change. Her lips stripped back off her teeth. Even in that position she struggled to lift the gun at me, screeching hatred. Hatred at me, who practically loved her. And honest to God it was an accident but my hands slipped. Her fingers unlatched or slipped or something, I don't really know anymore. I couldn't help it. Everything happened in a split-second blur. I swear it was beyond my control. My side suddenly gave out and my hand jerked away. It just happened. She slid back down screaming, wedging with a burbled shrill squeal into the millrace. She was howling dementedly with outrage. Her eyes glared up with pure hatred as she dragged the shotgun up against the force of the water. I removed my arm and edged frantically away from the wheel onto the crumbling platform. I swear my hand just slipped. Honest to God. And in the suddenness of her weight vanishing my flailing foot clanked the lever. Before I knew what was going on I heard the gears engage. It was a pure accident. Maybe I was trying to scrabble away from the coming blast of the shotgun. She gave one screech and the wheel lurched around. I heard it. Then there was only the moaning and whining sound of the big wheel's slow turning and turning. I lay there, gasping. The paddles had blood on, but only the first time around.

I'd *had* to roll over. She'd been lifting the gun at me again. You can see that. If she hadn't been trying to pull the trigger I'd have reached for her again. Accidents always happen when you're in a hurry. Everybody knows that.

I don't know how long it was before I dared look out. She was crushed beneath the wheel, her corpse deformed and mangled on the rocks and washed quite free of blood. The recesses between the boulders were covered with dark brown disks. I edged along the planking. The turning wheel had used Nichole to scrape the slab covering off the bed of the millrace. There were hundreds down on the river bed. I'd been right. Bexon had walled the lead coffin, now lying crumpled and exposed in the water, behind the millrace.

I could see Nichole's head in the clear water. It took me an age to work up the courage to lock the wheel again. Honestly, hand on my heart, it was accidental.

But as I climbed painfully down pity was alien to me. At that instant it was utterly unknowable. Her arm swayed like the limb of some obscene reptile as I splashed into the water below the waterfall. My side oozed blood.

I stood knee-deep in the millrace, the onrush thrusting against my legs. Looking around it became obvious most of the fortune was in copper and the occasional silver coins. I didn't blame Bexon, picking out the golds like he had and putting them in the Castle for bait. It was exactly the sort of thing I would have done. Anyway, the Romans considered copper the mediocre twin of gold itself. There was a small crusted bronze statue, a she-wolf suckling two infants.

I caught a glimpse of one dulled yellow. Her palm was tilted in the water, exposing a Roman gold between two fingers. I took it carefully from her.

"Hold them by the edge," I said. I keep telling people this but they take no notice.

I thought of saying something else to her submerged face through the rippling water layer, but finally didn't speak.

22

Janie was telling me off again.

"We didn't leave," she was saying angrily, "because a *polite* note from you was just too good to be true. You'd have just gone."

"Charming."

We'd all but packed. The bungalow stood clean and aired ready for more, for all the world like a runner on starting blocks before another race. I knew Janie was working up to something. She attacked suddenly in the lounge, unfairly bonny and colorful with white net gloves and pastel shades.

"Lovejoy."

You can tell it's trouble from the way they say things.

"Yes, love?"

"Look at me." I'd been staring admiringly at the hillside. St. Lonan's chapel with the valuable engravings was only two miles off and nobody would be there as early as this. I'd visited briefly. Some scoundrel would nick them one day. He could slip up the hedgerow, turn left at the road and cut through the sheepfold. Nobody'd see him. People are rogues and can't be trusted.

"Yes, love?" I gazed innocently into her lovely eyes. They looked full of suspicion. Women get like this.

"Lovejoy. The Roman coins."

"Don't," I got out brokenly.

"You didn't mention them very much to the police, did you?" She waited.

"They almost slipped my mind. When I heard how Nichole had been ... well, ill for so long, in close care and all that ..." I paused bravely. "Still, I did own up. Eventually."

"Did you take any?"

"Me? Take—?" I was outraged. "Certainly not!"

"Look at me, Lovejoy."

I'd accidentally turned away, honestly not because I wanted to avoid her eyes. I steadied up and gazed back.

"Did you," she asked, grim all of a sudden, "did you go back and steal some?"

I gasped, injured. Women have no sense of grief, not really. It takes a woman to be savage, even barbaric. Look at Nichole.

"Steal?" I demanded coldly. That hurt. "I showed the police where they were and everything. I said how I'd been looking for Bexon's find. And how she'd followed me and tried to keep the Romans for herself. Shooting me as soon as I'd found them. And pushing poor Edward off the cliff ..." I shuddered. No need to act for that.

"Steal," she said, still suspicious as hell, very determined. "Steal. As in nick, lift and thieve."

"No," I said, wounded to the quick.

"And," she added unabashed, "as in Lovejoy. There seemed very few coins. Only a dozen or so. Wouldn't a Roman army carry more than that?"

"How should I know?"

"Janie!" Algernon was suddenly there. I was very glad to see him. She never moved or took her eyes off me. "How *dare* you!" He quivered with indignation.

"How dare I what, Algernon?" Janie kept judging and weighing me up. She's basically lacking in trust. It must be terrible to be that way.

"Make—" he steeled himself—"well, what can only be designated ... *suggestions* about Lovejoy's character."

"Go and see to the car, Algernon," Janie said evenly. "I've business with Lovejoy."

"N—n—no, Janie."

She stared at him then, astonished. Served her right for losing confidence in her fellow man. She repeated her command but good old Algernon stood his ground quivering like a pointer.

"No, Janie. I can't allow these unpardonable insinuations against Lovejoy's character to go without demur."

"Algernon," Janie ground out. "I think it's time you faced the facts. Lovejoy's an unprincipled, greedy, lustful, selfish—"

Algernon scraped up some more demur and faced her, pale to the gills but still full of heroism.

"You're very—" he swallowed and finally made it "—wrong, Janie." I gasped in horror and turned aside, doing my strong-man-overcome.

"Algernon!" I exclaimed. "Janie didn't mean—"

"The swine's acting, Algernon!" Janie cried. "He's up to something. Can't you see?"

"If you only knew, Janie, what terrible events Lovejoy has been through," Algernon continued icily. "How absolutely courageous he was—"

"It was nothing," I muttered, embarrassed.

"How calmly he explained to the police, despite a serious wound—"

"It's only a scratch," I put in self-effacingly.

"—when he'd been in the very jaws of death!"

"Anyone would have done the same," I whispered nobly.

"I want a minute alone with him," Janie said angrily.

"I fully appreciate your—your relationship, Janie." Algernon drew himself up for a last stand. "Don't think I've failed to perceive your, well, your *weakness* where Lovejoy's concerned. I've turned a blind eye toward your—*goings-on* until now, perhaps even erroneously. But I must speak out."

I listened, marvelling. How can somebody reach twenty-two and still sound like Bram Stoker? He darted a kindly glance at me. I hastily looked courageous.

"I'm going to search him," Janie said sweetly. "From balls to bootlaces."

"I forbid it!" cried Bulldog Drummond.

184

"Then," she said, smiling to show she wasn't smiling at all, "I'm going to frogmarch him down to the Douglas police station and return the Roman things he's stolen."

"He's not stolen a single item!" Algernon stood firmly between us, dauntless despite having lost his cutlass in the first wave of boarders swarming over his galleon. "Your feelings are deforming your views. The very fact that your *obsessive desire* for Lovejoy is entirely *physical—*"

"Please," I said, broken. "I feel you are going too far."

"Your fatal attraction continually upsets your judgment!" he cried.

Even Janie was speechless at that. I couldn't help thinking Algernon was making some real progress.

"Don't think, Janie," he said with controlled calm, "I'm entirely ignorant of your repeated *surrenderings* to—well, what can only be called—*temptations of the flesh.*"

"Excuse me, please," I said quietly. "I—I can't stay to hear this."

"Stay here, Lovejoy!" Janie yelped.

The white-faced Algernon blocked her path as I trailed slowly and sadly to the door. "It's time I remonstrated, Janie," he was saying as I went, "on Lovejoy's behalf as well as your own. Have you never thought of your husband? Have you never searched in your innermost heart to learn what value a woman must place upon her sense of loyalty . . . ?"

Isn't education wonderful?

Outside I inspected the Lagonda's rear off-tire. You'd need a microscope to detect any change. It had taken me all bloody night. I scuffed the gravel in case there were telltale signs. Thank God, I offered up, for tubeless tires. Hiding stuff in those old-fashioned inner tubes must have been almost impossible.

I stuck my ear near the door. They were still at it.

"I'm going to search every ounce of his stuff before we move an inch!"

"And I absolutely forbid—!"

I looked again at the Lagonda. Anybody driving would have to take it slowly toward the main Liverpool ferry road. Especially on the bends, though the Romans were wedged thick and tight in layer after layer of unwaxed toffee paper and would be safe.

I'd left a lot of coins in the stream before climbing to the main road and phoning the police. Well, a dozen. I'd carried the main mass wrapped in my coat and stuffed it in an overgrown niche a hundred yards downstream for later. People have to learn they can't always have everything. I've had to. I would give two to the Castle's museum. Popplewell would have kittens. I'd insist they were exhibited with gold-lettered name cards, one blue, one green. They'd say: "These Roman treasures discovered in the Roman Province of the Isle of Man." I'd make sure the donors' names got pride of place, too: "Donated by Messrs. Dandy Jack, B. Manton and B. Wilkinson."

And if he asked I'd tell him B for budgie.

"He's a selfish—" Good old Janie, sticking at it.

Women can really get you down if you let them. What disappoints me most is how suspicious they are for no obvious reason. Even when you're being perfectly open they can't stop imagining what you might be up to. No trust in people. I'm glad I'm not like that.

It seemed a clear choice, Janie or the coins. Her, or a Roman treasure. The trouble is I can't stand disagreements. Women really like them. Ever noticed? Anyway, she probably had enough for the fare home.

I got into the Lagonda and drove off.